'Michelle Paver is a writer of extraordinary talent.
I was enthralled, from start to finish. To be back in
Michelle's world – with white fox mage riddles, ice bears,
tokoroth scars and mammuts – was a very special treat.
The storytelling was every bit as vivid and immersive as
I remembered and I was completely gripped by Torak
and Wolf's quest to the Edge of the World after Renn.
Michelle is in a league of her own with this series
and what luck for us all that she hasn't finished
with Torak, Renn and Wolf's world yet.'
Abi Elphinstone, author of *Rumblestar*

'A powerful invocation of a lost time and place that
will thrill young readers with a thirst for adventure.
To open the book is to place yourself into Torak
and Renn's Forest once again and be fully
immersed in their travels and trials.'
Jo Boyles, The Rocketship Bookshop, Salisbury

'In this stunning continuation of the *Wolf Brother* series,
Michelle Paver reminds us of the vital bond between
humans and Mother Nature. A pure delight for adults and
children alike, discover why booksellers, teachers and most
importantly readers adore Michelle Paver by entering this
living cave painting of a tale.'
Steve Bundy, Waterstones Manchester

'Paver's passion for nature, for wildlife, for the world's
wondrous wilds is an immersive joy.'
LoveReading4Kids

VIPER'S DAUGHTER

MICHELLE PAVER

ZEPHYR

an imprint of Head of Zeus

First published in the UK in 2020 by Zephyr, an imprint of Headof Zeus Ltd.
This paperback edition published in 2020 by Zephyr.

975312468

A catalogue record for this book is available from
the British Library.

ISBN (PB): 9781789542394
ISBN (E): 9781789542400

Typeset by Ed Pickford

Printed and bound in Great Britain by
CPI Group (UK) Ltd, Croydon CR0 4YY

Head of Zeus Ltd
5–8 Hardwick Street
London EC1R 4RG

WWW.HEADOFZEUS.COM

Also by Michelle Paver in this series

Wolf Brother
Spirit Walker
Soul Eater
Outcast
Oath Breaker
Ghost Hunter

For older readers

Dark Matter
Thin Air
Wakenhyrst

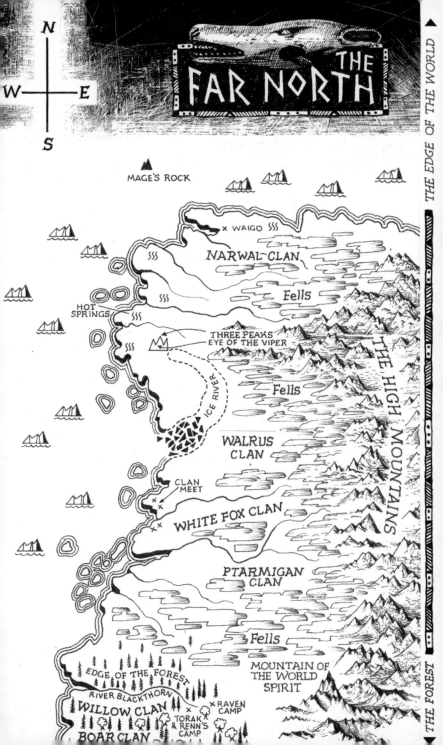

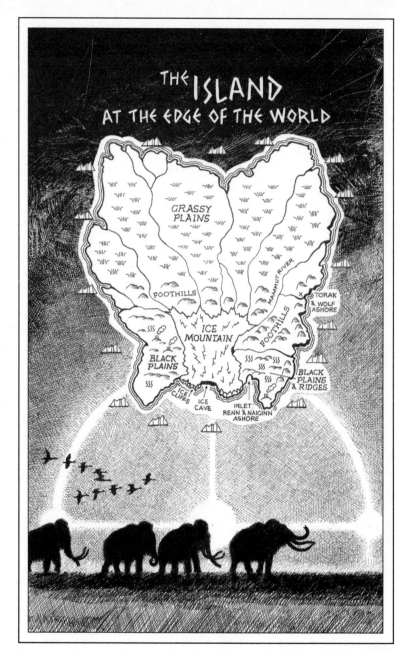

ONE

A bat flitted past Torak as he drew an arrow from his quiver. Wolf raised his muzzle and sniffed the breeze. He glanced at Torak, then into the thicket. *There.*

They crept between tangled alders, Torak squelching knee-deep in black water, Wolf's big paws making no sound. Torak picked a hair off a twig: coarse, reddish-brown. Elk calves are reddish-brown. The calf's mother must have hidden it in the thicket while she went to graze.

Torak glanced over his shoulder at the lake. Elk can swim deep underwater. She could be anywhere, diving to the bottom to uproot water lilies with her tongue.

Wolf froze: paw raised, ears rammed forwards. Dimly through the trees, Torak made out a calf-shaped darkness.

The calf whined and wobbled to its feet. It was as tall as a horse. One chop of its front hooves could split his skull.

As Torak nocked the arrow to his bow, Wolf gave a warning uff and the mother elk exploded from the lake in a chaos of white water and flailing hooves. Torak dodged. She cracked a trunk by his head. Wolf leapt and sank his fangs into her pendulous nose. She swung him high, he clung on. Torak couldn't get a clean shot, couldn't risk hitting his pack-brother. With a twist and a heave the elk sent Wolf flying. He hit a tree with a yelp. Torak floundered towards him. Mother and calf had disappeared into the Forest.

Groggily, Wolf lurched to his feet and wagged his tail. Torak gave a shaky laugh. 'That was close!' Renn would tease him when she heard how he'd nearly been brained by an elk.

As he was leaving the thicket he saw a Willow Clan hunting party, two women and two men, bearing a roe buck's quartered carcass. Wolf vanished into the Forest, as he did when strangers approached, but Torak put his fists to his chest in friendship. On impulse he asked if they'd seen his mate. 'Renn of the Raven Clan,' he called. 'She's been to see them but she's coming back today.'

One of the men turned, and in the dusk his clan-tattoos were stark: three willow leaves between his eyes, like a permanent frown. 'Saw her a couple of days ago,' he called back. 'Long way downriver.'

'Oh, then it wasn't her, the Ravens are camped *up*river.'

The man's frown became real. 'I know who I saw. Red hair, her uncle's Fin-Kedinn the Raven Leader. Summer before last she mated with the spirit walker, the boy who talks to wolves. That would be you.' His eyes narrowed and he touched a bone amulet on his jerkin: *Stay away.*

'Looked like she was going on a journey,' a woman sneered. 'She was paddling a canoe, had a pack and a sleeping-sack.'

Torak bristled. 'Then it definitely wasn't her.'

The woman sniggered. 'Maybe she's tired of you.'

Laughing, they went on their way.

Torak was still irritated when he reached camp. It was in darkness, no welcoming firelight and no Renn.

Neither Wolf nor his mate Darkfur had returned from the hunt, but the cubs pounced on Torak, leaping at his chest and whining for food, while their older brother Pebble gave him a distracted greeting. Pebble took his cub-watching duties seriously and rarely relaxed.

In the shelter Torak found the double sleeping-sack as he'd left it, although slightly chewed. He felt a twinge of unease. It was the Cloudberry Moon, when parts of the river were still choked with salmon – and salmon means bears. Renn said Torak worried too much about bears. Torak said she would worry too if her father had been killed by one.

Ah, but she could look after herself, she was the best shot in the Forest with a bow and arrow. She'd be annoyed if he went to find her.

The wind rose, blowing thistledown in his face like summer snow. The pines stirred restlessly. They knew something was wrong.

Tracking was what Torak did best, and even by starlight he found Renn's three-day-old trail. To his alarm it didn't lead towards the valley where her clan was camped, but down to the River Blackthorn where he and Renn kept their canoe. The canoe was gone. Drag-marks and bent twigs told him that Renn had paddled downriver, just as the Willow man had said.

She was going on a journey. She had a pack and a sleeping-sack.

This was all wrong, it couldn't be Renn. She would have had to make that gear in secret: scraping and sewing reindeer hides for the sleeping-sack, weaving willow withes for the pack. She would have had to deceive Torak for days.

No, no, it couldn't be true. Renn wouldn't do that. She wouldn't leave him without a word.

But she had.

Many Lights and Darks ago when Wolf was a cub, his father and mother and pack-mates were drowned by a terrible Fast Wet. Wolf had been frightened and hungry until Tall Tailless had come. They'd been pack-brothers ever since.

Tall Tailless wasn't a *real* wolf, he walked on his hind legs and had neither fur nor tail – but he had the heart and spirit of a wolf and he was part of the pack. Together he and Wolf had hunted their first deer. They'd fought demons and other bad things. They'd found mates. But even though Wolf was one breath with his mate and cubs, he'd always known that it was his purpose to be with Tall Tailless and protect him. This was what Wolf was *for*.

The Hot Bright Eye was rising in the Up as Wolf and his mate trotted back to the Den with their bellies full of salmon. The cubs attacked them with eager snuffle-licks and hungry whines, *Me first! Me first!* Jostling, shoving, they gulped the delicious sicked-up fish, then collapsed in a pile and fell asleep.

Wolf's mate lay with her muzzle between her paws, and even the older cub snoozed – but Wolf was restless. Something wasn't right, he felt it in his fur. The pines guarding the Den were moaning. What had they sensed?

Now Wolf felt it too: a shadow and a threat, some creature in the Forest that didn't belong. He caught no whiff of demon, but his flanks throbbed from old wounds, and suddenly he *knew* – with the strange certainty that came to him at times – that Tall Tailless needed him.

As Wolf raced uphill to catch the scents, his keen ears caught the sounds of the Forest: a lynx sharpening her claws in the next valley, two stallions fighting many lopes away – but where was Tall Tailless? Wolf swerved to avoid a bear clawing an ants' nest. The bear lashed out, Wolf dodged with scornful ease. He wasn't afraid of bears. He wasn't afraid of anything except losing his pack-brother.

At the edge of the cliff he skittered to a halt. Far below, the Fast Wet foamed angrily between rocks. Tall Tailless sat on a log, pushing himself through the wet with a stick.

Wait for me! Wolf barked. But his pack-brother's ears weren't as keen as his, he didn't answer.

Wolf put up his muzzle and howled: *Wait – for me!*

Tall Tailless howled a reply: *Go back to the Den! You can't come!*

Wait! howled Wolf.

You can't come!

Wolf was stunned. Tall Tailless was leaving the pack? *Leaving Wolf?*

Wolf ran in circles, mewing in distress. A wolf does not abandon his pack. *Tall Tailless could not leave.* But neither could Wolf: he had to look after his mate and cubs.

And yet Tall Tailless *needed* him. Wolf didn't know what to do.

His mate appeared in the bracken, panting, her black flanks heaving. *Go,* her bright eyes told him. *The older cub will take turns with me to hunt and watch the young.*

Wolf ran to her and touched noses. *I come back.*

I know.

Wolf couldn't find a way down the cliff, and the Fast Wet was carrying Tall Tailless away. Wolf raced along the cliff-top, leaping logs, splashing through bogs. He was falling behind. In desperation he scrambled over the cliff edge and slid, digging in his claws, bashing into thornbushes.

The Fast Wet swept Tall Tailless round a bend.

Wolf lost his grip and fell head over paws off the cliff.

Long after Wolf had been left behind, his anguished howls still rang in Torak's ears. He *hated* leaving Wolf, but he couldn't ask him to abandon Darkfur and the cubs and they couldn't come too. Torak had to travel fast to have any chance of finding Renn. If only he'd been able to make Wolf understand – but how could he, when he didn't understand himself?

He'd set off the moment he'd discovered the canoe was gone, struggling on foot along the thickly wooded riverbank. No point returning to camp, he always carried what he needed to survive: axe and knife, bow and arrows, slingshot; waterskin, strike-fire, tinder pouch, sewing kit, medicine horn. He'd made little progress, and when he'd found a Boar Clan dugout in the shallows he'd taken it. Stealing a boat is almost as bad as stealing an axe. Torak told himself he could make amends later.

The dugout was ridiculously clumsy, nothing like the nimble deerhide craft he'd made with Renn. At times he paddled through a choking stink of salmon, the shallows clogged with rotting fish and black with ravens. Rip and Rek weren't among them. Torak hoped they'd gone with Renn: ravens are wary, very good at warning of danger.

He also passed bears, but they were too busy feasting in the light summer night to trouble him. A family of otters rose on their hind legs to watch him go. Their fur glinted with fish scales, reminding him with a pang of Wolf's fishy breath when he'd been hunting salmon.

At daybreak Torak found an inlet where Renn had camped. He knew it was her by the tiny flakes of flint where she'd sharpened an arrowhead, and her footprints were as familiar as his own.

Rainwater in her tracks, a fox's paw-prints crossing the ashes of her fire: she'd camped here two nights ago – and made no attempt at concealment. She knew Torak was too good at tracking to be fooled.

Or did she *want* him to follow? Maybe she'd left him a sign? When they were apart they sometimes kept in touch by scratching marks on the pale undersides of horsehoof mushrooms; the marks quickly turned brown and didn't fade.

Torak found plenty of mushrooms on tree trunks, but no marks underneath. Distractedly, he scratched the scar on his forearm.

Renn's sign shouted at him from a boulder in the shallows: a raven's foot chalked in white, pointing upriver. *Turn back. Find the White Raven.*

Torak chewed his lip. Why tell him to seek their friend Dark?

This was hopeless, Renn could be anywhere. She could have hidden the canoe and headed on foot for any of the countless valleys of the Open Forest, or for Lake Axehead or the Deep Forest or the Mountains or the Sea. Without knowing *why* she'd left, he was travelling blind.

He began to be angry. Come on, Renn, this isn't funny. Nevertheless, he decided to follow her sign.

Struggling against the current was hard work, and as the day wore on his shoulders began to cramp. Mist filled the valley. Dusk crept up the pines. He shivered. No warmth in his eelskin jerkin and knee-length leggings, and this summer he hadn't bothered to make boots. Barefoot and without a sleeping-sack wasn't the best way to start a journey, especially in the northernmost part of the Forest.

At last he glimpsed a white raven in a willow, a sure sign that Dark was nearby. As Torak hauled the hated dugout up the bank, the bird greeted him with an echoing ark! and flew into the Forest. Torak followed her to his friend's camp, in a dim glade guarded by watchful birch trees.

Dark sat by his fire with his Mage's drum on his knees. On it he'd scattered the little slate creatures he loved to carve: aurochs, beavers, vipers. His strange white head was bent and he was making the creatures dance by tapping the drum with a swan's thighbone. He'd set a salmon to roast and ground a pouchful of earthblood; a pile of the crumbly dark-red stone lay beside him and he was covered in reddish dust. Ark had taken on a pink tinge as she perched on his shoulder, busily preening her feathers.

At Torak's approach, Dark raised his head. For a moment his pale eyes were as remote as mountains. Then he saw who it was and his face lit up.

Torak stepped into the firelight.

Dark's smile faded. 'Ah. So she's gone.'

Torak stared. 'You *knew?*'

Dark sucked in his breath.

'What's this about?' cried Torak. 'Where'd she go?'

'I don't know where. But I think I know why.'

TWO

Torak prowled the glade, slashing bracken with a stick.

'You knew and you didn't tell me.'

'Renn asked me not to,' said Dark.

'You're supposed to be my friend—'

'She's my friend too—'

'Keeping secrets? Talking behind my back?'

'It wasn't like that! And stop hitting the bracken, you're frightening Ark.'

Strangers meeting Dark saw an odd-looking boy with long white hair and eyes like a sky full of snow. They mistook his gentleness for weakness, but soon realized their error. He'd been born without colour and abandoned by his father when he was eight. For seven winters he'd survived on his own in the Mountains, his only companions a white raven he'd rescued from crows, and his sister's ghost. Two summers ago the Raven Clan had taken him in and made him their Mage. He was still getting used to living with people in the Forest, and sometimes he went off for a few days alone to clear his head.

Torak flung away the stick and glared at the fire. 'Tell me why she left.'

With his knife Dark speared a salmon eye and offered it. Torak scowled, so Dark ate it himself. 'She said things kept happening that she couldn't explain.'

'What things?'

'A spring-trap she forgot to warn you about. And that time she nearly shot you when you were hunting.'

'Those were accidents.'

'She didn't think so. She said, "There's something inside me that wants to hurt Torak."'

'*What?* Renn would never hurt me!'

'I know. But she's terrified that she might. She said she has to find out what it is and make it stop. She thinks – ' his voice dropped – 'it might have something to do with her mother.'

The birch trees whispered in alarm. The white raven crested her head-feathers and croaked. Torak met Dark's eyes. 'But the Viper Mage is dead.'

'I know, but that's what Renn told me.'

Torak rubbed his hand across his mouth. 'And you've no idea where she's gone?'

'She said the signs all point one way but she wouldn't say

where. I've been seeing signs too. And just now my drum told me something weird: *The demon that is not demon—*'

'I don't have time for Mage's riddles.'

'And I keep seeing tusks.' He pointed at a tree where he'd left a small slate weasel as an offering. Shadows of twigs had given it horns. 'I see them in clouds, in eddies in the river: huge twisted tusks, much bigger than a boar's—'

'I don't *care* about tusks, I need to find Renn!'

'But, Torak, they're linked! The tusks have something to do with her, I can feel it.'

'Do a finding charm, do it now.'

'She doesn't *want* you to find her. That's why she left without telling you, because you'd insist on going too and she couldn't take that risk!'

'Just do the charm!'

Dark opened his mouth – then shut it. 'I don't need to. Look at the sky.'

Above their heads the First Tree glowed luminous green. Its shimmering branches held the moon and the stars, and its unseen roots trapped demons in the Otherworld. Torak felt the hairs on the back of his neck prickle. The First Tree shone brightest on dark winter nights and rarely showed itself in summer. It had appeared for a reason. He saw from Dark's rapt expression that he thought so too.

As they watched, the green lights faded till all that remained was a single shining bough arching like a vast arrow across the deep blue sky.

'North,' said Torak. 'It's telling us she's gone north.'

'A long way north.'

Torak glanced at him. 'You don't mean the *Far* North? She'd never try that on her own.'

'Even further. I can feel it.'

'But what could be further than the Far North?'

Ark cawed a greeting, and they saw Fin-Kedinn at the edge of the glade.

Leaning on his staff, the Leader of the Raven Clan limped towards them. Silver glinted in his dark-red hair and his short straight beard. Firelight carved his features in shadow and flame. 'Beyond the Far North,' he said, 'is the Edge of the World.'

手手

Dark set a log by the fire and Fin-Kedinn sat, putting his hand to the old wound in his thigh. His one-eared dog sniffed the salmon, then caught Fin-Kedinn's glance and lay meekly at his feet. Dark sat too. Ark flew to a tree and glared at the dog.

Torak stood, clenching and unclenching his fists. The Far North was an icy, treeless waste ruled by the north wind and haunted by great white bears. He and Renn had been there once. They'd been lucky to escape with their lives. 'Tell me about the Edge of the World. Have you been there?'

Fin-Kedinn shook his head. 'But when I was younger I

hunted in the Far North with the White Fox Clan, they told me what they knew.'

'So now you can tell me.'

'First you must eat.'

'I'm not hungry—'

'You look as if you haven't eaten in days. Sit. Eat. You too, Dark, and while you're eating, tell me about Renn.'

When Fin-Kedinn spoke, people obeyed. Torak flung himself down and glowered at the fire.

He discovered he was ravenous and fell on his share of the smoke-blackened salmon while Fin-Kedinn listened to Dark. He was Torak's foster father, but he hadn't greeted him as he usually did by touching foreheads. Torak wondered if Fin-Kedinn blamed him that Renn was gone.

Dark finished speaking. Fin-Kedinn turned to Torak. 'And Renn never told you anything?'

'Nothing,' muttered Torak. Twice he'd woken in the night to find her staring into the dark, but he'd thought she was missing her clan. She preferred to camp near them, while he loved living with the wolves in the lonely valleys. Sometimes they'd fought about that.

'You never sensed something was wrong?' Fin-Kedinn's voice was sharp.

'Are you saying it's my fault that she left?'

'Are you?'

Torak met his vivid blue freezing stare. 'I thought we were happy,' he said. 'Tell me about the Edge of the World.'

15

The Raven Leader held his gaze a moment longer. 'None who seek it have ever returned. But it's said that the Sea pours endlessly into the void. Stories tell of an island near the edge. Its rivers boil, its mountains spew fire. It's guarded by the spirits of huge creatures who died long ago.'

Torak swallowed. 'How do you reach it?'

Fin-Kedinn lifted his broad shoulders. 'The old stories say it's across the Sea, beyond the northernmost cliffs of the Far North.' He turned to Dark. 'That's why I came to find you. After you told me of your visions, I remembered something. The Narwal Clan hunts along that coast. Their speech is different from ours and they build their shelters from the bones of huge hairy monsters as tall as trees – and from their tusks.'

'I've seen such creatures in my dreams!' cried Dark. 'But I can never sense where they live! They don't seem to belong anywhere, not to the Forest, the Mountains or the Sea – how can that *be*? They have to live somewhere.'

'They belong to the Deep Past,' said Fin-Kedinn. 'They lived during the Great Cold, but the ancestors killed too many, and they died out. Now and then, a Narwal hunter finds a carcass frozen in the earth. These ancient creatures are sacred. Narwals call them *mammut*.'

Torak jumped to his feet and slung his quiver over his shoulder. 'Well, if they all died out, we don't need to worry about them.'

Fin-Kedinn faced him across the crackling heat. 'You're not going after her.'

'She's got four days' lead, I'm not waiting any longer.'

'How about trusting Renn to know what she's doing?'

'I do trust her. I'd trust her with my life. But something is driving her to the Edge of the World and whatever it is, she isn't going to face it alone.'

THREE

The north wind rushed screaming over the fells, savaging the Forest and warning Torak back. Before him the desolate shore and the sounding Sea, ahead the empty lands – and beyond them the Far North, where ice bears hunted people as if they were prey. Renn was heading there alone.

Until he'd met her Torak had never had a friend. For five summers they'd shared secrets and danger. The flash of her dark-red hair in the green Forest lit his spirit as nothing else could.

He'd made it to the mouth of the river in a day, Fin-Kedinn having relented and given him his own deerhide canoe, saying he'd return the stolen dugout to the Boars. Too exhausted to build a proper shelter of saplings, Torak carried the canoe into the Forest and upended it. He would sleep beneath, and he wanted a last night under trees.

After hastily waking a fire for company, he checked his gear. Flint-tipped arrows, spare bowstrings of braided deer sinew, pebbles for his slingshot. He stuffed thistledown in his tinder pouch, made needles of split gull bones from a skeleton on the shore, and slotted them into his wingbone needle-case. He would hang everything on his belt, in case he capsized.

He'd need an eyeshield too. Though it was summer, Fin-Kedinn had warned of icebergs, and Torak had been snow-blind. It had felt as if someone was rubbing grit in his eyes. Muttering thanks to a birch tree, he peeled a strip of bark and cut two eye-slits. A while back he'd lost his head-band, but he wouldn't bother making another. If the circle tattooed on his forehead disconcerted people, too bad.

Dark had given him his sleeping-sack and beaver-hide boots, as well as some dried salmon cakes and a thick coil of auroch-gut sausage – but these he would save for the journey. He found burdock stems and horse mushrooms and munched them raw, spitting out maggots.

As an offering he tucked a piece of mushroom in the fork of a rowan. 'Forest,' he prayed. 'You've helped me all my life. Help me find Renn. Keep her safe.'

But what power could the Forest have in a treeless land ruled by ice, wind and waves?

The light was beginning to die. The clans know that this is when demons lurk, hiding in darkness, breathing malice

19

and despair. Demons are hard to see, and you rarely catch more than a glimpse at the corner of your eye. Renn had a Mage's sense for them and Wolf knew when they were near. Torak had come to rely on them both.

Dark had given him a pouch of ground earthblood: 'You can trade it for warmer clothes on the coast, but keep some on you always.'

'You think I'll need it?' Torak had asked.

The demon that is not demon. I don't know what that means, but earthblood might protect you. May the guardian fly with you, Torak.'

'And with you.'

Torak filled his medicine horn and dabbed earthblood on the small slate wolf he wore at his neck, and on the greenstone wrist-guard which Fin-Kedinn had made for Renn and she'd given to him.

He lay in Dark's sleeping-sack, watching the glimmer of firelight through the canoe and trying not to think of the double sleeping-sack he'd shared with Renn.

He touched the scar on his forearm. He'd got it when he was twelve summers old, the night the demon bear killed his father. He remembered running from the wreck of the camp he'd built with Fa. Collapsing against an oak tree, staring numbly into its branches. For the first time ever he'd been truly alone. He was alone again now.

Beyond the creak and murmur of the Forest he heard the endless soughing of the Sea. He hated to think of Renn paddling north at the mercy of the Sea Mother, who lives in the deeps and is beyond good and evil: who kills without pity or warning.

An owl hooted. Embers crackled. Wolf called fire 'the Bright Beast-that-Bites-Hot' because he'd burnt his paw when he was a cub. Torak missed him: the ticklish warmth of nibble-licks, the meaty smell of his big rough pads. He missed everything that was mysterious and unknowable about his pack-brother. Wolf came and went as silently as mist. His ears were so keen he could hear the clouds pass, his nose so sharp he could scent the breath of a fish. If Torak was merely thinking of setting off on a hunt, Wolf would open his amber eyes: *Let's go!* Sometimes Wolf knew how he felt before he felt it himself…

Torak woke to the certainty that he was being watched. It wasn't some inquisitive badger, the Forest was quiet. Too quiet.

Silently drawing his knife, he crawled from under the canoe. He rose to his feet. The brief summer night was nearly over. The Forest was full of shadows.

A spruce branch tapped a warning on his shoulder. He turned.

A magpie lit onto a branch, showering him with dew. He breathed out. The feeling was gone.

On the beach he startled a pair of oystercatchers, who flew in circles, loudly scolding him for getting too near their nest. Behind him the Forest was a wall of darkness. Ahead, Sea and sky were a dismal grey blur.

Trees, rocks, river and Sea: they'd all seen Renn pass, but they weren't telling. Torak's spirits sank as he thought of the days ahead, seeking a girl who didn't want to be found.

Wolf appeared silently, as wolves do, and stood on the rocks thirty paces away. Dew beaded the silver fur on his flanks, the black fur on his head and shoulders, his russet-rimmed ears. Normally he would have bounded to Torak and greeted him with tail-lashing and rubbing, licking and nuzzling. When he didn't, Torak halved the distance between them and sat on a mound of dried kelp.

Wolves don't only speak with howls and grunts and whines, but with their whole bodies. Although much of wolf talk is subtle and easily missed, it was plain what Wolf was saying. His tail pointed stiffly at the sky and he was staring stonily at the Sea. *You left me. I'm cross.*

Torak couldn't speak wolf as well as a real wolf: he couldn't apologize by sleeking back his ears and tucking his tail between his legs. Kneeling, he uttered a low grunt-whine. *Sorry.*

Wolf twitched one ear and went on staring at the Sea. *Still cross.*

Torak sat next to him. He rubbed his shoulder against Wolf's. Wolf slammed him with his hindquarters, knocking him into the kelp. He growled and soft-bit Torak's upper arm, worried it, released it without a mark.

Torak noticed a fresh scab on Wolf's left foreleg. He shot Wolf a glance. *How?*

Fell.

Sensing embarrassment, Torak didn't ask more.

Some things take ages to say in person talk, but a wolf can say them in a tail-flick; others he can't say at all. Torak couldn't explain why Renn had left, or where they were heading. He could only tell Wolf that the pack-sister was many lopes away and he missed her.

Wolf leant against him and licked his chin. *Me too.*

A wolf does not abandon his pack. Torak knew what a wrench it had been for Wolf to leave Darkfur and the cubs. Burying his face in his pack-brother's scruff, he sniffed Wolf's well-loved smell of sweet grass and warm fur. He felt the tickle of whiskers and teeth as Wolf gently nibbled his ear. He felt better than he had since Renn had left.

I am with you, said Wolf. *We find the pack-sister together.*

The Demon sneers at the fawning wolf and the trembling boy. They are anxious and frightened. Flawed, imperfect, weak.

All living creatures are weak. The Raven Leader is weak because he rules his clan by persuasion, not force. The girl is weak because she is a Mage, yet fears to wield her power. The boy is weak because he loves the girl. The Demon despises love. Love is weakness. It makes the living easy to control.

Now boy and wolf are back in the Forest, the boy gathering his gear, the wolf sniffing the canoe. The wolf is able to smell lesser demons – the slinkers and scurriers – but it cannot smell the Demon.

23

The Demon is cleverer and stronger than all living things. It hates and hungers for their shining souls, it longs to grind and shred, to feel them thrashing and shrieking in endless pain...

But the Demon cannot feed – for the Demon is not free.

The Demon must be free.

The Demon shall be free.

fOUR

The seal knew it was too big for Renn to kill. As she paddled nearer, it went on basking on the iceberg, while behind it a flock of kittiwakes settled for a rest.

A sunny day, a calm Sea – but suddenly the seal hoisted itself off the ice and slid under the waves. Renn heeded the warning and swerved. The kittiwakes shot mewing into the air as the iceberg tipped over with a crash, sending a wave that nearly swamped the canoe.

While Renn struggled through rocking shards of ice, the kittiwakes landed on a distant blue floe. Seabirds can rest anywhere, she could not. She'd hardly slept in days and was losing track of time. As she'd followed the coast north, she'd passed snow-covered mountains and vast silent valleys. No Forest to protect her, and no night: the cold white sun never set.

The strip of shingle under the cliffs was scarcely wide enough for the canoe, but she couldn't put it off any longer. She'd been relying on her eyeshield as a disguise. She had to go further, or risk some meddlesome hunter wondering what a girl from the Forest was doing in the Far North.

Rip and Rek swept past, scattering the kittiwakes. The ravens were making cuckoo calls. Renn wished they wouldn't, it only heightened the strangeness of this strange land.

Hating what she was about to do, she crouched in the shelter of a rock. On a stone she ground lichen with dried elderberries from the Forest, mixed them with seawater in her birch-bark baler, combed the black dye through her long red hair. The wind chilled her scalp. Despite her reindeer-fur clothes she shivered.

Next she must hide her Raven clan-tattoos: the three blue-black bars on her cheekbones. In a clam shell she blended wood-ash with deer fat and smeared it on her face, as if she was mourning the dead.

Now for her clan-creature feathers sewn down the side of her parka. She couldn't bear to remove them, so she covered them by sewing sea-eagle feathers on top. Finally she used the last of the dye to paint the back of her hand with the four-toed mark of the Sea-eagle Clan.

'There,' she said shakily. 'You're not Renn of the Ravens. You're Rheu of the Sea-eagles.'

She'd chosen the Sea-eagles as they got on with

everyone, but it didn't help. Never had she disguised herself so completely. She'd betrayed her clan and disrespected another, and by changing her name she'd gone even further. *Your name is yourself held in a sound. If you change it, you change your luck.*

But what else could she do? Torak would come after her. She had to make sure he didn't find her.

A seal bobbed up in the shallows. It was the same one who'd warned her about the iceberg: wise brown eyes, bushy whiskers like a gruff old man. It gave her a penetrating look and dived, flicking up its tail-flippers. It didn't like what it saw.

Renn whistled for Rip and Rek. The ravens dropped down from the cliffs – then veered off with startled caws: *Rap! Rap! Stranger!*

'I'm not a stranger, it's me!'

But they were gone. They didn't know who she was.

The mourning marks were stiffening on her cheeks. She felt sick. Her name-soul was coming loose. For comfort she wound Torak's headband around her temples. She wondered if he'd guessed that she'd taken it. She'd needed something of his to keep her company.

Water was lapping her boots: the Sea Mother was breathing out, sending in the tide. *You can't stay here.*

As Renn pushed off, she saw a face in the water. The girl who stared back at her had long black hair and pale, stern features. She didn't recognize herself.

She had become her mother: Seshru the Viper Mage.

27

'You are not your mother,' Dark had told her.

'But I have her marrow in my bones. Maybe that's why this is happening.'

'You don't know that.'

'I saw a viper in a rowan. Vipers don't climb trees.'

He blew stone-dust off the pine marten he was carving. 'When I was born, my mother named me Swan Clan. I don't like being Swan, they abandoned me. But I can't change who I am. I can only change what I do.'

'Your mother wasn't a Soul-Eater. She didn't kill people.'

He looked at her through his cobwebby hair. 'Is she why you haven't done Magecraft for two summers? You're still afraid of becoming like her?'

'I don't *need* to do Magecraft—'

'You're wrong.' His severity made her blink. 'People need healing, Renn, they need help finding prey. If we all refused to do Magecraft, how would the clans live?'

'There's something inside me that wants to hurt Torak. I have to find out what it is and make it stop.'

'Magecraft could help you do that.'

'I don't need spells to tell me where to go, I see signs wherever I look!'

'Be careful, Renn. Magecraft is a force, like a river. If it's held back it turns dangerous.'

Maybe he was right. But a few days later she'd had the dream that had forced her to leave. Standing in a cave of ice, holding Torak's heart in her hands...

She woke with a jolt, slumped over her paddle. She had to find a campsite or she'd fall overboard.

It had been winter when she'd been here last, the Sea frozen, the land a howling wilderness of snow. She'd been shocked to recognize nothing. Even keeping the coast on her right was hard, all these rocky islands littering the Sea like flakes of flint dropped by the World Spirit sharpening his axe. Without the North Star to guide her she'd reckoned by the sun, and when she couldn't see it, by the stunted bushes cowering from the wind.

That was one thing that hadn't changed: the power and anger of the wind. With no Forest to stop it, it came rushing down from the mountains to attack the fells, where dwarf willow and birch flattened themselves against the ground, and even rocks huddled together.

The sun became fierce, soon Renn was sweating under her clothes. When the sun went in she would be chilled, and a White Fox hunter had told her once that it isn't cold that kills, it's wet.

She passed cliffs clamorous with seabirds and reeking of droppings. Nowhere to camp. In the next bay a grey whale lay rotting on the shore. The stink was stomach-churning, yet still she hesitated – until a great white bear ambled from behind the carcass, snuffed her scent and glared.

Clouds hid the sun and it started to snow. In the Far

North the weather changes with unnerving suddenness: spring, summer, autumn and winter in a single day.

She reached a black beach strewn with icebergs. On a ridge above the tideline she spotted three hunched boulders that might provide shelter.

The ridge was taller than it had appeared from the Sea. She was standing beneath it when she noticed there were *four* boulders. There had only been three.

She glimpsed movement. She edged away.

The Hidden People live in rivers and rocks, and they look like us except when they turn their backs, which are hollow as rotten trees. They hate being seen and you must take care not to anger them by camping too close to their rocks.

Renn put her fist to her heart and bowed. 'I'm sorry, I'll go.'

A fifth boulder appeared. No, not a boulder: a creature she'd never seen before. As big as a bison and immensely shaggy, its lugubrious brown face was flanked by massive downwards-curving horns. It was moulting, blond wool clotting its humped shoulders and hanging almost as far as surprisingly small, neat hooves.

Renn had heard about musk-oxen from Dark. 'If you keep your distance they probably won't attack. Although they're very bad-tempered so sometimes they do. It's fine to gather their wool snagged on bushes, but don't ever hunt them. They belong to the Hidden People.'

Renn stepped backwards. 'I'm not after your prey,' she told the dwellers in the rocks.

The musk-ox snorted. It lowered its head and pawed the ground.

She raised her hand. 'Look: I'm walking to my canoe.' A second musk-ox appeared. Then three more. They stood in a row, staring at her amid clouds of breath.

She floundered through mounds of kelp. The musk-oxen leapt down from the ridge as nimbly as deer and moved towards her.

'I'm sorry!' she shouted, digging in her paddle.

Balefully they watched till she was gone.

The snow turned to sleet, stinging her face and trickling inside her reindeer-fur mittens. She was beginning to despair of finding a campsite when she came to a bleak islet with a lake shivering in the middle.

Dizzy with exhaustion, she hauled the canoe behind some rocks by the lake – having first checked that they were rocks, not musk-oxen. She didn't sense any Hidden People, but she couldn't be sure.

The sleet eased. Clouds of midges whined in her ears and crawled up her nose. She'd eaten all her Forest food, so she trudged down to the Sea with her fishing gear, baited her hooks with limpets and set her lines.

Renn knew the ways of the Sea, she'd been fostered with the Whale Clan when she was nine; but only now did she remember that if you mix things from the Forest with those of the Sea, you risk offending the Sea Mother.

Every piece of her gear came from the Forest: her yew-wood bow and dogwood arrows, her reindeer-fur parka and leggings, beaver-hide boots, sleeping-sack, pack, canoe. Her fishing-hooks were thorns lashed with spruce root, the lines horse hair, the floats pine bark. The only things that *wouldn't* offend the Sea Mother were the bait and the sink-stones.

Biting her lips, she pulled in the lines and trudged up to the lake to start all over again. She knew she wasn't thinking straight. Her head was buzzing with fatigue. She should have set the lines in the lake to begin with.

No driftwood on the shore but plenty of bones: the blotchy skull of a bear, the white skeletons of seals. After waking a fire she smoked her clothes and gear to make their scent less Foresty. She ate a handful of mussels off the rocks and some slimy kelp. Unwrapped her bow, polished it with hazelnut oil from the horn in her medicine pouch. 'At least I've got you,' she mumbled. She still missed her old bow which Fin-Kedinn had made for her, and she gave this one lots of attention so it wouldn't feel left out.

Clumsily she overturned the canoe, piled stones against the sides and wriggled underneath. Grey daylight seeped through the deerhide. Ice clinked in the shallows. Behind it the immense silence of the Far North.

Rip and Rek had not come back. She had relied on them to warn her of danger – but why should they now, when she'd shunned her clan? She pictured demons and Hidden People emerging from the rocks. Ice bears swimming stealthily ashore.

It was too painful to think of Torak, so she thought about

32

Wolf and Darkfur at the river, teaching the cubs to hunt. Salmon were good prey for beginners, no nasty antlers or hooves to hurt small bodies.

Unwinding Torak's headband, she sniffed his smell of sweat and wolves and pine-blood. By now he must have found out why she'd left. But did he know how much she hated doing it? How fiercely it hurt?

She saw him coming after her. She saw his long dark hair and lean brown face with its Wolf Clan tattoos: two dotted lines along his cheekbones, with the thin scar cutting the left one to cancel it out. She saw the green flecks in his light-grey eyes from when he'd spirit walked in trees.

Would he ever forgive her for lying to him?

She was woken by wingbeats, a splash and the honking of swans. The scar on the back of her hand was itching. Her fingers felt gritty. When she wriggled out of her sleeping-sack, a stub of charcoal crunched under her knee.

The sun lay low on the amber Sea. In the fire a piece of birch bark was smouldering. Someone had scratched Torak's forest mark on it in charcoal, over and over in anger. With a cry Renn grabbed the bark and flung it in the lake. She'd broken the spell just in time: if the fire had eaten even one of those marks it might have done Torak great harm.

To her horror, her hands were black with charcoal. 'I didn't do it,' she cried. And yet who else was there? And where would you find birch bark and charcoal in a land without trees?

Running to the Sea, she scrubbed her hands.

Her fishing lines were back in the shallows. That wasn't right, she'd put them in the lake. Yet here they were – and they'd caught something.

A sob rose in her throat. It was the whiskery seal. It was dead.

This was her fault. Now she had to cut up the carcass and use every part. Baring her teeth, she drew her knife and slit the fat grey belly. She sprang to her feet. From the mess of guts slid a viper. It hissed and vanished into the kelp.

This can't be happening, thought Renn.

A figure sat by the fire with its back to her. As Renn edged closer, the figure turned and she saw the beautiful, heartless face of her mother.

'You're dead,' said Renn. 'You were killed three summers ago. I watched you die.'

Seshru's black lips twisted in her sideways smile. 'So?'

FIVE

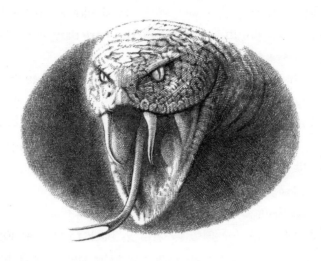

'What *are* you?' whispered Renn.

'Don't you know?' taunted Seshru.

She sat cross-legged by the fire, slowly pouring ash from palm to palm. She was barefoot, in a sleeveless tunic of silver sealskin, and though snow fell thickly, none touched her long dark hair or her smooth pale arms. The Viper tattoo on her brow was a vertical line of arrow-heads set point to point, and her dark-blue gaze held Renn's with the fixity of a snake. 'Interesting disguise,' she remarked. 'You look better with black hair. Like mother, like daughter.'

'You're not real,' said Renn. Putting out her hand, she passed it through her mother's face as if it were smoke.

'Are you sure?' The Viper Mage blew on the embers, loosing a flurry of sparks. One burnt Renn's cheek. 'If I'm not real, how could you feel that?'

Renn shielded her face with both arms, exposing the zigzag tattoos on her wrists that warded off evil. 'You're dead. I saw you die.'

Seshru's shoulders shook with silent laughter. 'You keep saying that!'

'I hated you when you were alive, I still do. You broke my father's heart. If he hadn't gone looking for you he wouldn't have died on the ice—'

'Your father was weak.'

'You wanted to put a demon in me and make me your tokoroth: your creature, to obey your every command.'

'And now look at you,' sneered her mother. 'A snug little mated pair with your wolf boy! Although we both know that's not perfect. You want to be with your clan. He can't wait to leave. It'll never work.' Flicking out her pointed black tongue, she tasted Renn's unease. 'And now you've left him, as I left your father.'

'I had to, he was in danger—'

'Yes, from you. All that rage bubbling inside you.'

'I'm not angry with Torak.'

'Really? Those "accidents" in the Forest? That charm just now, burning his mark?'

'You're behind this. That's why you're here.'

Her mother's gaze slid sideways. 'A snake can still bite when you cut off its head. But what intrigues me is that you never confided in your wolf boy. You're good at secrets. You get that from me.'

'I get nothing from you!'

More noiseless laughter. 'Daughter, why fool yourself? You can run all the way to the Edge of the World, it'll never be far enough! You can't run from what's in your marrow.'

'Why are you here?' Renn said coldly.

'*Finally*, you ask why! That's good, that's what Mages do.'

'I don't need praise from you.'

The Viper Mage regarded her. 'Do you remember the day I died? You knelt beside me as I lay with an arrow in my breast. Your face was wet—'

'With rain, not tears.'

Seshru smiled. 'Oh, I know! You'd have shot me yourself if someone hadn't beaten you to it.' Again she poured handfuls of ash. 'People were frightened, they didn't dare come near me. But not you and the wolf boy. You heard what I said as I died. *This is not the end...*'

'What do you mean?' Renn's voice cracked. 'You're dead. The Soul-Eaters are dead, so are their tokoroths. You don't exist!'

'There will come a time when you'll wish I did: when you'll wish you were only up against me. At least I was human.'

'Is that why you're here?' snarled Renn. 'To warn me?'

'What do you think?'

What *was* this woman – this thing before her? Renn's thoughts flew to the day she'd put the Death Marks on her mother. The smell of wet earthblood as she drew the circles on Seshru's forehead, breast and heels to keep her souls together. Hadn't the Death Marks worked?

If Seshru had lost her name-soul she would be a ghost. If she'd lost her clan-soul she'd be a demon. If she'd lost her world-soul she would have snapped her link with trees, hunters and prey – she would be drifting for ever beyond the stars...

'I'm not a Lost One,' said Seshru as if Renn had spoken aloud. 'And I'm not a demon or a ghost.'

In a supple movement she rose and spread her hands, and at her command the ash lifted and whirled around her in a glittering cloud. Her hair was a writhing mane of serpents. Her empty eyes pierced Renn's.

'You're a dream,' said Renn.

'Well *done!*' mocked Seshru. 'But don't you know what that means?'

The ashes blew apart. Seshru was gone. 'It means I'm inside you,' she hissed in Renn's head. 'You can't ever be rid of me. I'm part of who you are...'

Renn woke standing by the dead fire. Clouds hid the sun. Wind roughened the surface of the lake.

The Viper Mage was gone, but her venom lingered. Renn was shaking. Her hands were black with charcoal. A piece of birch bark floated on the lake. It bore traces of Torak's marks. So that part had been real: she must have scrawled them in her sleep and laid the bark on the fire.

Was it possible her mother was right? That deep down she *was* angry with Torak and wished him harm?

'No,' she said aloud. 'No. *No!* You'll never make me believe that! I'd never hurt Torak!'

At the lake she cupped water and drank. She filled her waterskin. Her fishing lines were here in the lake, after all. She'd caught nothing, but she spotted a ptarmigan in the rocks and shot it.

When you make a kill, you must thank the prey and use every part of it. This is the Pact, the oldest law of all: hunters must treat the prey with respect, and in return the World Spirit will send more prey.

Renn thanked the bird and wished its spirit peace. She tucked the innards under a stone as an offering and ate the liver and heart raw. She skinned the body and legs and roasted them, then to save time she wrapped the bones in the feathered skin and put it on the other side of the lake. Soon afterwards an eagle swooped and carried it off. Renn took that as a good sign.

Honouring the Pact steadied her, but she couldn't forget what Seshru had said. *This is not the end.* What had she meant?

At the shore Renn braved the cold and took off her parka and leggings, then scrubbed every trace of the dream off her skin with wet kelp, which she threw in the shallows. Having dressed, she ate the ptarmigan.

Her mother's great skill had been to make people believe her lies. Well, not this time. Renn would not be turned from her purpose. Whatever was trying to hurt Torak – be it a demon or something else – she would find it and make it stop. And if that meant going to the Edge of the World, that was what she would do.

She had an idea. Spreading her long hair on a rock, she took her knife and cut it short. She tied Torak's headband round her temples. There. Now her face in the lake was nothing like her mother's.

Hair holds part of your world-soul, so you mustn't let it fall into the wrong hands. Renn tied hers around a stone and lobbed it into the Sea. It would come to no harm there, and it might make amends to the Sea Mother for her gear and the deerhide canoe.

A sleek grey head poked out of the water and shook its extravagant whiskers. Renn smiled. 'I'm glad you're all right. Sorry I killed you in my dream.'

The seal rolled over and floated on its back. In its front flippers it held a scarlet crab which it proceeded to munch. Renn hoped this meant the Sea Mother had forgiven her for the canoe.

The Sea-eagle 'tattoo' on her hand had faded a bit, so she renewed it with lichen, then rubbed more ash on her 'mourning marks'.

Her disguise didn't feel quite as wrong as it had before. She still had her raven feathers under the others, and her medicine pouch was raven skin (it's against clan law to kill

40

your clan-creature, but she'd found a dead one in the Forest).
In the pouch was the tiny bag she'd sewn before she left,
which held tufts of underfur from Wolf and Darkfur and a
milk tooth from each of the cubs. On a thong at her neck
hung the duckbone whistle which Torak had whittled for
her last summer. When she blew it she heard no sound, but
Wolf could hear it, and so could Rip and Rek.

Renn blew it.

At first she caught nothing but the hiss of wind in marsh
grass. Then a powerful swish of wings – and Rip lit down
and greeted her with a bow and a throaty gurgle. Rek
perched on her shoulder and ran a lock of her hair gently
through her bill. The raven was no longer disconcerted
by her disguise.

'Greetings, little guardians,' Renn said with a bow.
'Glad you've realized I'm still me. Please don't stay away
again.'

The fog arrived without warning, creeping up on her as
she paddled north. Within moments it was so thick she
couldn't see the end of the canoe.

When it thinned, she was startled to see how far she'd
drifted from the coast. She tried to turn, but the current
wouldn't let her. It was a flat, pale green, nothing like the
choppy blue water she'd just left, and it was trying to drag
her out to Sea.

'Don't fight it!' called a voice. 'Turn level with the shore and keep going, you'll be all right!'

Renn did as he said.

Through the shifting whiteness she made out a hunter in a long grey skinboat. 'Not far to go, you're nearly clear!' he shouted.

He was right. Feeling a bit foolish, she shouted her thanks. The Whale Clan had taught her about riptides. 'I can't believe I forgot what to do!'

Grinning, he paddled closer and threw back his hood. 'You probably don't get many riptides in the Forest.'

He was about her own age and quite extraordinarily handsome. His fair hair hung in many braids about his shoulders, and his light-blue eyes were striking in his wind-burnt face. His clan-tattoos were two fine black lines from the corners of his mouth to his jaw, and he maintained a respectful distance as he held up his palm in friendship. 'I'm Naiginn of the Narwal Clan. I can tell by your speech that you're from the Far South. What name do you carry?'

Renn hesitated. 'I'm Rheu of the Sea-eagles.'

To her relief it no longer felt wrong. Her name-soul was secure. Inside, she was still Renn of the Raven Clan.

SIX

Torak swerved to avoid a lump of black ice and Wolf nearly fell overboard. Torak growled at him to sit, but Wolf ignored him. His eyes were bulging and he was panting in alarm.

To reassure him, Torak stretched and yawned. It didn't work. It had taken a lot to persuade Wolf into the canoe and he still hated it. He was scared of the Sea and he kept hearing giant fish howling in the deep.

Fin-Kedinn had warned Torak about whales. 'In summer they swim close to the shore to scratch their bellies. And if you see seabirds screaming above a patch of Sea, stay clear, it means whales are feeding beneath.'

Twice a whale had surfaced so close they'd nearly capsized, and a while ago the wind had done its best to smash them against an iceberg. It was a warning. The Far North was telling them to go back to the Forest.

As the sun didn't set in this strange land, Torak had lost track of the days. He was gripped by the fear that he would never find Renn. He couldn't imagine being without her. Even when they were with others, they had only to exchange a glance across the fire to feel the bond between them. What if that never happened again?

He was also sharply aware that while she had prepared for her journey, he had not. He needed warm, seaworthy clothes and a skinboat made of whale bone and seal hide that wouldn't anger the Sea Mother, but so far he hadn't met anyone to make the trade. He knew people lived here: the Ptarmigans, the Narwal and Walrus Clans, his friends the White Foxes. Where were they all?

To make matters worse, his waterskin was empty, and though the cliffs scowling down at him were veined with waterfalls, he couldn't find anywhere to land.

From a sea-cave ahead came a weird, booming roar – although from what Torak could make out, there was nothing inside but boulders. What sort of land was this where even boulders roared?

Wolf's ears were flat against his skull, his tail clamped between his legs. Uff, he warned.

Three of what Torak had thought were boulders lumbered into the Sea and swam towards them, spouting spray. They swam fast. A huffing snort off the prow and a head bobbed up. The creature was covered in warts and

44

from its pouchy upper lip jutted two sturdy yellow tusks as long as Torak's forearm. Its dark eyes were harder than pebbles.

Fin-Kedinn had warned him about walruses too. 'They don't eat people but if you get too close they'll kill.'

'I'm not hunting you,' Torak told the walrus. With a grunt it dived, displaying a mottled bulk twice the size of the canoe as it sank out of sight.

Its companions had also vanished. Uneasily, Torak and Wolf peered into the dark-green water. The walruses could be anywhere.

He hadn't paddled far when they bobbed up again, some distance behind. Rearing above the waves, they stared at Torak until he'd paddled well past their cave.

By now he was desperately thirsty and Wolf's flanks were heaving. They came to a stream crashing down a cliff with a strip of shore beneath, but as Torak paddled towards it, Wolf growled. His hackles were stiff and he was gazing intently at the clifftop. Torak craned his neck and locked eyes with the biggest ice bear he'd ever seen.

She stood high above, her long claws gripping the edge. Her chest and muzzle were stained yellow with blubber, her nose criss-crossed with scars. Her flat black stare never left Torak as she tasted his scent with her dark-grey tongue.

Clumsily, he paddled backwards. The ice bear shifted from paw to paw, seeking a way down to this temptingly easy prey.

Two fluffy white cubs appeared either side of her and peered curiously at Torak. Their mother swung her long neck. Obediently they backed out of sight.

Snuffing, licking the air, the bear extended one massive forepaw and clawed for a foothold. Pebbles skittered and bounced. She drew back with a hiss. Too steep. Torak sped off before she changed her mind.

His hands on the paddle were slippery with sweat. He had encountered ice bears before, and he knew the raging power of their blood-hunger. To an ice bear, *all* other creatures are prey.

And summer was their leanest time. In winter they hunted seals hauled out on the frozen Sea – but now there was no sea ice, which meant fewer seals and hungrier bears.

As Torak paddled north, white patches dotting the land took on a sinister significance. Was that driftwood on the shore, or a sleeping bear? Was that ice on the fells? Was it?

Passing a headland, he saw a bear amble into the Sea. He slowed, straining to see which way it swam. Only the very top of its head showed, and the slightest wave hid it from view. He *thought* he spotted it swimming south, but as he dug in his paddle the sun came out and every glinting wave became a bear.

He was glancing over his shoulder for the tenth time when a shuddering jolt nearly pitched him overboard. Too late he saw the black iceberg lurking under the waves.

The canoe crumpled like an eggshell and the Sea rushed in.

Torak huddled naked in a cave above the shore, teeth chattering uncontrollably as he hacked a strip off his sleeping-sack for a foot-binding. Wolf was leaning against his back to warm him up, while in front he was scorchingly close to the blaze he'd woken from a pile of driftwood.

He was lucky. The Sea Mother had spat him into the shallows, taking the canoe and his boots but sparing his life. He still had his weapons, gear and the pouch of earth-blood. He was going to need it more than ever.

His jerkin and leggings hung from stakes, dripping onto the flames. When he put them on they were still damp, so he tied them off at elbows and knees with a spare bowstring and stuffed them full of grass. It was scratchy and crawling with insects, but it would keep him alive.

No one in the Far North travels overland in summer, and no one wears eelskin clothes. Too bad. He hadn't met anyone to make a trade and he didn't have time to stop and make better gear for himself.

The wind nearly knocked him over as he made his way onto the fells, ripping the warmth from his flesh and making his skull ache. Wolf slitted his eyes but didn't feel the cold: already his underfur was thicker, his pelt as fluffy as if it was winter.

The ground turned marshy and the wind went off to maul someone else. Midges swarmed. Wolf bounded across the bog and sat furiously scratching while Torak jumped grimly from tussock to tussock. He sank into sticky black mud, yanked his foot free. It came away without his foot-binding. Same with the other.

Sweaty and midge-bitten, he finally reached firmer ground – and the wind came roaring back. This was hopeless, he was still within arrowshot of the shore. The whole of this horrible treeless land was against him: wind, Sea, walruses, ice bears, the earth itself.

For the first time since leaving the Forest, he was angry with Renn. They had shared everything together. At times they'd laughed so much they'd cried. At others they'd spoken of their fathers and how deeply they missed them. How could she *do* this?

A shadow slid over him. He gasped. The wind was so strong he could barely stand, and yet the great white owl hovered perfectly still.

In the past, Torak had been forced to kill a snow owl. Seeing one now made him feel guilty. He was glad when it glided away across the fells.

Wolf had run ahead and was nowhere in sight. Torak felt eyes on him and turned.

Two skinboats were rocking in the shallows. Each was manned by four boys about his own age, in parkas and leggings of stained grey hide. All had the flat round wind-darkened faces of the people of the Far North and all were scowling at him.

Warily he raised a hand in greeting. One boy jabbered something that sounded like a clatter of stones. The others sniggered.

Torak realized he must look ridiculous with his clothes stuffed full of grass: like the clumsy turf men the ice clans raise to honour the wind. 'My name's Torak,' he called. 'Can you understand me?'

The boy who'd spoken squared his shoulders. Even from a distance he stank of rancid blubber. His face was shiny with it, his eyes permanently slitted against the wind. His clan-tattoos were two black lines from mouth to chin, like a grimace. 'Orvo.' He struck his chest with his fist. 'Narwal Clan. What are you?'

Torak didn't feel like explaining about being clanless so he said he was from the Forest in the south. 'I have earth-blood to trade for clothes and a skinboat. Can you help?'

The boy called Orvo stared as if he'd asked for the moon. 'You want a *skinboat*?'

'I said I'll trade.'

'Narwals don't trade skinboats.'

'All right. Maybe someone else will. If not, I'll walk.'

Orvo spoke to the others in his own speech and they burst out laughing. '*Walk?*' jeered Orvo. 'Walking's for women and Softbellies!'

Torak looked at him. 'What's a Softbelly?'

'You, from the Far South! Get in the boat.'

'Why?'

'That's the rule: strangers go to the Boat Leader. He's my uncle,' he added proudly. 'Don't worry, Softbelly, he won't hurt you. He'll just send you back south. You're not tough enough for the Far North.'

SEVEN

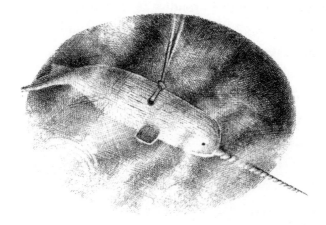

The Narwal boys took Torak's weapons and hustled him into Orvo's skinboat. As they headed north, Torak spotted Wolf following on land. The Narwals didn't notice.

They passed a bay where a gaggle of younger boys toiled up and down, dragging what appeared to be rocks roped to their waists. 'Walrus skulls,' muttered Orvo. 'When they're older they'll drag a boulder, then a whale skull.'

'Why?' said Torak.

'It's the rule.'

Torak asked how come he spoke Southern, and Orvo said it was a rule that someone had to, to trade with other clans. The Narwals had lots of rules. Boys must be raised by their uncles instead of their fathers, because uncles punished more harshly. When the first frosts came they had to sleep in the open, and stand at the edge of the Great Crag to conquer fear. 'And when my father's father got too old to hunt,' he boasted, 'I had to watch the elders strangle him.'

'*Why?*'

'To make me strong. The weak die, the tough survive. Softbellies like you wouldn't last long.'

'Why do you call us that?'

'Because you're weak. You can't even eat our food.'

'How do you know? I've never tried it.'

Orvo bared his teeth. 'You will!'

Torak's silence seemed to annoy him. 'Don't you have rules in this "Forest" of yours?'

'Not as many as you. What's the point?'

'It keeps us alive! Hunting whales is dangerous! Six men in a boat must act as one! Don't your people hunt whales?'

'There aren't any in the Forest.'

Orvo snorted. 'Must be a poor place.'

'It's where your driftwood comes from.'

'No, it isn't, driftwood comes from the Sea.'

'Yes, but before that it was trees.'

Another snort. 'What are these "trees"? I don't believe in them! Driftwood is giant kelp from the Sea!'

Torak gave up.

They rounded a headland into a swirl of woodsmoke and the stench of middens, and he saw hundreds of shelters strung along the coast. This was where all the people had been: they were gathered for a clan meet.

Orvo said that as Narwals and Walruses were 'Sea hunters', they got the best campsites on the ridge by the river. The Ptarmigans, who hunted reindeer and hare, took the boggy ground, while Softbellies like the Kelps had to camp near the dungheaps. Torak asked if there was anyone from the White Fox Clan, but they were putting into the shallows and there was no more time for talk.

The noise was overwhelming. Men haggling over piles of eider ducks and blocks of mashed, dried berries. Women scrutinizing hides for holes, sniffing skins full of whale oil, prodding sides of smoked reindeer. The boys jostled Torak past racks of wind-dried cod and he came face to face with the strangest fish he'd ever seen. As big as a man and weirdly flattened, both its bulging eyes were on the same side of its head.

'Halibut,' said Orvo. 'Don't you have them in your "Forest"?'

Torak ignored that.

The Narwal campsite was at the far end of the clan meet, and weirdly silent. No talk, no laughter. Even the dogs were subdued. Above the shore towered five pairs of whales' jawbones, each supporting a skinboat that could take six men. A boy ground charcoal with blubber, an old man painted a walrus on a boat, probably for hunting luck. He was missing three fingers; Torak guessed from frostbite.

On the shore, bare-chested Narwal men butchered a walrus while women toiled over the skin. The walrus had the thickest hide of any creature Torak had encountered.

The women had laboriously split it through its thickness, stopping just before the other end and opening it out, to double it in size. They were scraping it clean with flakes of black flint, and would cure it by rubbing in the creature's mashed brains, piled nearby.

Torak saw another woman standing in a rawhide vat of urine, kneading a seal hide with her bare feet. Her companions were making rope, cutting hide in spiral strips and chewing to render it pliable. All the women had cropped hair, long maggot-eaten robes and grim expressions. At Orvo's approach they shuffled fearfully out of his way.

A girl with a withered arm wasn't quick enough and Orvo would have struck her if Torak hadn't grabbed his shoulder. 'She didn't do anything!' he protested.

Angrily Orvo shook him off. 'A half-man gets out of the way, that's the rule!'

'A what?'

'A half-man, a female!'

The girl looked about ten summers old. She resembled an anxious squirrel, with pouchy cheeks and prominent teeth half-hidden by a bone disc that hung from her pierced upper lip. She stared at Torak as if she couldn't believe he'd tried to help her. She was still staring as he followed Orvo to the Narwals' shelter.

This was a massive tent of split walrus hides criss-crossed with ropes lashed to boulders. Above the entrance was fixed a tusk as straight as a spear; Torak guessed it was that of a narwal.

'This shelter's only a summer one,' muttered Orvo. 'The camp of our ancestors at Waigo is much bigger.'

Torak had never heard of any clan naming a campsite. He was thinking how odd that was when he saw what was planted on a stake by the shelter: the bloody, fly-blackened head of a wolf.

His world tilted. Then he noticed that this wolf's muzzle was white, its teeth worn to stumps. He turned on Orvo. 'Why would you do this? What harm did this old wolf do you?'

Orvo bristled. 'Demons hide in wolves. Everyone knows that!'

'Nonsense, wolves *fight* demons!'

'What do you know about wolves, or demons? Get inside!'

The horror of the slaughtered wolf stayed with Torak as he crawled after Orvo into the shelter. In the Forest it's forbidden to kill a hunter – but not in the Far North. It had never occurred to Torak that this meant they might kill wolves.

He found himself in a chilly outer chamber: Orvo said it was where the half-men slept. Torak bumped against a stack of barbed bone harpoons. 'Don't touch,' warned Orvo. 'They're poisoned.'

They pushed past a heavy walrus-hide hanging, into the men's chamber. It was bigger and warmer, musk-ox pelts strewn around a driftwood fire. From the smoke-hole dangled a carved narwal of polished bone about a hand long. It swam amid waves of blue smoke. Orvo knelt before it and touched his forehead to the ground.

Through the fug Torak saw six bare-chested, blubber-smeared men sitting cross-legged in the gloom. Their faces were purpled by wind and cold and their clan-tattoos gave them permanent scowls. All were beardless, with one or more red dots tattooed on their chins; a pock-marked man in the middle had seven. Orvo said each dot meant that the man had killed a whale, and the pock-marked man was his uncle, the Boat Leader. The boy was whispering: he'd left his swagger outside.

The Boat Leader barked at him in their stony speech and Orvo turned to Torak. 'He says we eat first, then talk.'

Two girls crawled in dragging a bulging sealskin, then shuffled out. The Boat Leader slit the skin with his knife, and he and the others pulled out fistfuls of dark-red slime. 'Eat,' Orvo urged Torak with his mouth full.

'What is it?' said Torak.

'*Kivyak*. We pack a sealskin with guillemots and seal flippers and leave it to rot for the summer. Eat!'

They were watching him: he could see the challenge in their eyes. He scooped a gooey handful of rancid fat and clotted blood. The smell made his eyes water. He crammed it in his mouth. Forced it down. Burst out coughing.

The Narwals roared with laughter and scooped more *kivyak*, sucking and munching with exaggerated relish: *See how tough we are!*

Already Torak was feeling dizzy. In the Forest the clans

brewed drinks that had the same effect as this rotten meat. He always avoided them, he didn't want his souls to wander. It seemed that for the Narwals, getting drunk was the point.

'My uncle says you're not eating enough.' Orvo's speech was slurred. 'He says you're weak, like all Softbellies.'

Torak told him to ask if he could trade earthblood for a skinboat.

'He asks why you want to go north.'

'I'm looking for my mate.'

'Who took her?'

'No one took her, she left.'

This provoked cries of outrage. 'If one of our half-men left, we'd kill her!'

'That's not our way,' said Torak.

'You're even weaker than we thought! Go back south! Get a new mate!'

Torak struggled to keep his temper. 'Have you seen her? She has red hair and she's seeking the Edge of the World.'

This enraged the Boat Leader. He thrust his face at Torak, spattering him with *kivyak*. 'No Softbelly may seek the Edge of the World!'

'Why not?'

'This would anger the spirits of mammut!'

'Mammut,' cried the Narwals, touching filthy fingers to the walls.

For the first time Torak saw that they were covered in paintings of strange lumpy creatures. Their legs were as thick as tree-trunks, their massive tusks curved out and then in again, and their long thin noses snaked all the way to their stumpy feet. *They belong to the Deep Past*, Fin-Kedinn had said. *But the ancestors killed too many and they died out. Occasionally a Narwal hunter finds a carcass frozen in the earth. These ancient creatures are sacred: Narwals call them* mammut.

The Boat Leader was ranting, dangerously drunk. Orvo was struggling to keep up. 'Far over the Sea from Waigo lies the Island no Narwal has ever seen! They say that fiery cracks gape on the Otherworld, and only the spirits of long-dead mammut keep the demons inside! You will sleep now, Softbelly, then you will slink back to your Forest — and you will go on foot!'

Arguing was pointless. Torak watched the men gobble the last of the *kivyak*, then pass out one by one. He curled up on the other side of the fire and slid into evil dreams.

He dreamt that Wolf hung skewered on a stake, accusing him with dead white eyes: *You should have warned me, pack-brother.*

'It's only a dream,' Renn whispered in his ear. She lay in front of him with her back against his chest. 'I missed you,' he murmured, breathing her wonderful sharp junipery scent. He bent to kiss her spine, but instead of the little smooth bumps that he loved, his lips touched slimy rotten flesh...

He woke with a shudder.

The wind had risen, the walls of the shelter were slapping noisily. The Narwal men lay on their backs, snoring. The roof could have fallen in and they wouldn't have woken.

No point stealing weapons and a skinboat, they'd only catch him. And he couldn't ignore that dream. Wolf's head on the stake: *Should have warned me, pack-brother.* He had to find Wolf and tell him to stay away or the Narwals would kill him.

As Torak crawled into the icy outer chamber, he had to pick his way around sleeping women. Only the girl with the withered arm was awake, furtively plucking maggots from a chunk of putrid meat and cramming them in her mouth. When she saw Torak she froze.

Signing her to silence, he slipped out to warn Wolf.

The Thunderer was growling in the Up and the Great Wet was clawing the shore. Lemmings and rock-squirrels scurried for their burrows. Wolf had to find shelter too – but he was *hungry*. And there were lots of fish near the great dens of the taillesses. Wolf had known since he was a cub that taillesses are very like wolves. They live in packs and hunt to feed their families, they're clever, they love talking and playing, and sometimes their young do foolish things and get killed. But unlike wolves, taillesses sleep for ages – which makes it easy to steal their fish.

Wolf was seeking a way past the dogs when he saw Tall Tailless running towards him. No time for greetings, Tall Tailless told Wolf to get away *now*, or the taillesses would kill him.

Wolf was astonished. Taillesses don't hunt wolves. But his pack-brother meant it, so he went.

By now the Thunderer was roaring in the Up, the Great Wet attacking the shore with huge white paws. Wolf had to find shelter fast.

He hadn't gone far when he spotted a hollow in the bank above the Fast Wet. As he scrambled in he smelt prey. Yes, prey buried in his hollow, and deliciously rotten.

Wolf began to dig, thrusting aside the frozen earth with powerful forepaws. He forgot the howling wind and the Thunderer's fury. He smelt that this prey was bigger than the biggest bison – and very, *very* old.

Lightning flared and thunder cracked. The World Spirit slashed the sky and rain pelted down, soaking Torak.

The wind was savaging shelters and ripping boats from their moorings. People were hurrying to rescue their belongings, but at the Narwal camp nobody stirred.

One of their skinboats had been torn from its arch, it was rolling along the shore like a birch-bark toy. Frightened women huddled outside the shelter, but there was no sign of their men, who were still sleeping off the *kivyak*.

Torak crawled inside and grabbed Orvo's shoulder. 'Wake up! You're losing your boats!' The boy curled into a ball and scowled in his sleep. Torak crawled out again, shouted at the women to help. They didn't understand, or maybe they feared to obey a Softbelly.

Floundering through mounds of slippery kelp, Torak went after the boat. Someone ran up behind him. The girl with the withered arm was strong for her size, and determined. Together they overturned the boat and flung in rocks to weigh it down, then struggled back to the other boats. The girl fetched rope. As she and Torak fought to secure the first craft, Orvo emerged blinking from the shelter.

'Get more rope!' yelled Torak.

Orvo dived back inside and returned moments later with the men.

By the time the storm had blown over, all the boats had been saved, although the one on the shore had a rent that would take days to repair. Women brought dry clothes for the men, but when the girl with the withered arm offered Torak a dry parka, the Boat Leader sent her running with a glare. He hated being beholden to a Softbelly. Torak would get no thanks for saving the boats.

He was trudging towards the shelter when a woman jabbered in alarm and pointed inland. The men ran for their weapons. Torak's belly turned over.

Wolf hadn't fled for the fells, he was halfway up the riverbank, well within arrowshot as he tore at a half-buried carcass.

'Don't shoot!' yelled Torak, flinging himself in front of the men.

'Out of our way!' shouted Orvo. 'We have to kill the demon!'

Torak put his hands to his mouth and howled. *Danger! Run!*

Wolf was gone in a flash, flying like a grey ghost over the fells. The Narwals' arrows thudded harmlessly into the bank.

All eyes turned on Torak. Within moments he was surrounded by a thicket of spears.

'You *talked* to the demon,' said Orvo.

'He's not a demon, he's my pack-brother!' But he could see they didn't believe him.

Over his shoulder he saw the carcass which had nearly killed Wolf. A leg like a tree-trunk ended in a huge round foot. A gash in thick earth-coloured hide revealed flesh as dark as horse meat. But this was no horse.

Torak thought fast. 'Orvo, tell them this proves Wolf is no demon! No demon would go near mammut, let alone eat it!'

But the Narwals had seen for themselves. *'Mammut,'* they muttered, touching their foreheads as they hurried past Torak to dig out the sacred remains.

They were still at work when he saw a man on the shore walking towards him. As fat as a well-nourished seal, the man had a black stripe tattooed across his nose, which marked him as a member of the White Fox Clan.

Torak ran to meet him. 'Inuktiluk!' he cried.

The older man grinned. 'I just heard you were here!'

Turning to the Boat Leader, he had a brief exchange in Narwal. Then to Torak: 'They might seem ungrateful but you've won their respect. He says you can have a skinboat and a safe-passage stick for you and Wolf as far as Waigo. You're lucky, they rarely give those to anyone.' His grin widened. 'And before you ask, yes, Renn passed this way. And she sends you a message.'

EIGHT

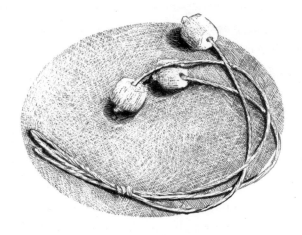

'What did she say?' cried Torak. 'Is she all right?'

'Patience!' chuckled Inuktiluk. 'She was here not two days ago—'

'Only two days?'

'She'd lost her way among the islands, it slowed her down.'

'What did she *say*?'

'I don't know, I was out fishing. Tanugeak saw her.'

'Where's Tanugeak?'

'Picking mushrooms on the fells, she'll be back soon.'

Torak let out a roar. To the White Foxes 'soon' could mean anything from a day to half a moon.

Inuktiluk clapped him on the back. 'You're too thin, Torak. You need to be fat to survive up here, I've told you before. Come and eat while we wait for Tanugeak.'

The White Foxes were camped at the other end of the clan meet. Children chased each other round the shelter of brown-and-white seal hide, and sled-dogs, recognizing Torak's scent, sprang up with yowly greetings. Inside, Torak found himself in the cheerful din of a White Fox daymeal. Tanugeak wasn't back.

It was a relief to be with people who enjoyed eating and laughing. White Fox boys weren't forced to drag walrus skulls, and when they got into scrapes their elders simply ignored them till they came to their senses. White Fox hunters happily jumbled up prey from land and Sea, and men and women got along as equals. Inuktiluk smiled at the Narwals' belief that they were better than everyone else. 'The sun doesn't give them any more light than the rest of us!'

Torak realized he was hungry. He wolfed a bowlful of reindeer fat whipped with crowberries and herring livers, and a crunchy pale-green mess pickled in seawater that Inuktiluk called roseroot.

Soon the others returned to the clan meet, leaving the two of them alone. While Inuktiluk ladled willowherb tea into kelp beakers, Torak put on the warm clothes they'd given him, his eelskin ones having been taken and fed to the dogs.

He was chewing a slab of oily black whale meat when a short, plump woman crawled into the shelter. She wore a cape of blue teal feathers and her belt jingled with tiny bone carvings from all the people she'd helped. Her brown face was creased with laughter lines and she had the bright, slanted eyes of her clan-creature. She gave Torak a friendly, penetrating glance.

He stopped eating. 'Tell me everything,' he said to Tanugeak the White Fox Mage.

'She doesn't want you to find her,' Tanugeak said calmly.

Torak blinked. 'That's all she said?'

'There's a reason she cut off her hair and dyed it black. There's a reason she goes by the name of Rheu of the Sea-eagles. Don't be angry with her.'

'I'm not.'

'Anger is a form of madness. It won't help either of you.'

'But she must have told you something!'

Tanugeak glanced at Inuktiluk. 'She asked me to read the signs, to find out where she should go.'

'And?'

'I had a message from the people beyond the clouds. From the dead,' she explained. 'I told Renn, so I'll tell you. *To find what you seek, you must put the island of wings to flight and cross the forest in the treeless land. You must save the past by burning the present.*'

Torak groaned. 'I hate riddles!'

Tanugeak smiled. 'That's what Renn said.'

Torak could hear exactly how she'd said it. He missed her so much it hurt. 'Why did you let her leave?' he burst out.

'"Let"? You sound like a Narwal! Renn chose to leave. Why are you scratching that scar on your arm?'

'Because it's itchy.'

'How did you get it?'

'A bear. Which has nothing to do with—'

'Show me.' After taking his forearm in her plump hands, she drew a chip of yellow stone from her medicine pouch and crumbled it to dust in her fingers. It smelt sharply of rotten eggs as she rubbed it on his scar. 'We call this bloodstone because when it burns it leaves a scarlet stain. I'll give you some. It helps against demons and fleas.'

'You don't think I should go after her,' Torak said accusingly.

'What good would it do?' put in Inuktiluk, who until now had listened in silence.

'Look at me, Torak,' said Tanugeak.

Reluctantly he met her bright, steady gaze.

'How long since you spirit walked?'

'Not for two summers. But—'

'In your eyes I see traces of souls not your own.'

'That's what happens when you spirit walk,' he said impatiently. 'But that's in the past. You have to help me find Renn!'

'It's not easy to put the past behind you. I told Renn the same thing. She didn't listen either.'

'I can't go back to the Forest without her.'

'But it's more dangerous for you.' She touched her collar

of white feathers. 'My spirit guide is the snow owl: the guardian of the Far North. It doesn't want you here. I don't know why. Do you?'

Torak thought of the snow owl he'd killed. He shook his head.

Tanugeak sighed. 'If you survive, it'll be by doing what you do best: by thinking like other creatures.'

'More riddles,' he growled.

'No, just common sense.'

'Renn will be all right,' said Inuktiluk. 'Naiginn will look after her.'

Torak looked at him. 'Who's Naiginn?'

The White Foxes exchanged startled glances. 'You didn't know?' said Tanugeak.

'Know *what*? Who's Naiginn?'

'A young hunter of the Narwal Clan,' said Inuktiluk. 'He and Renn arrived together. They left together too. But surely the Narwals told you that?'

'You've no reason to be jealous,' said Tanugeak. 'We know Naiginn. Renn's safe with him.'

'Oh, I'm sure,' snarled Torak. 'I've seen how Narwals treat women!'

'Naiginn's different,' she insisted. 'He doesn't even look like them, his mother wasn't from the Far North. When he was a boy his father sent him to us to learn our ways.'

'I fostered him myself,' said Inuktiluk. 'He's brave, clever and the best hunter in his clan.'

Somehow that didn't make Torak feel any better.

'Naiginn knows the Far North,' said Inuktiluk.

'Meaning I don't.'

'You were here in winter for less than a moon, in summer it's a different world! How would you help Renn if you got trampled by a musk-ox or eaten by an ice bear?'

Torak glowered at the fire. What was Renn doing with a stranger, even if he was the best hunter in his clan?

The tent flap was flung back and Orvo put in his head. 'I've brought your skinboat.'

Torak shot him a look. 'This Naiginn: why didn't you tell me he'd been here with my mate?'

'That was for the Boat Leader to say, not me.'

Torak blew out a long breath. 'Inuktiluk, Tanugeak: thank you for your help but I can't go back to the Forest. I'm going north.'

The skinboat was a one-man craft of split walrus hides sewn with sinew and stretched over a light whalebone frame. It reminded Torak of Seal Clan boats, except that it wasn't covered at bow and stern. Orvo solemnly showed him the baler, rope and fishing gear stowed under the cross-struts. He explained that the hides were those of female walruses, as females didn't fight, so their hides weren't weakened by scars. 'Now and then you must rub it with snow, or it'll crack when you hit ice – and you will hit ice. Here, these are for you.'

He held out Torak's axe, knife and slingshot, the safe-passage stick, and a driftwood bow with a quiver made of woven kelp. The arrows it held were fletched with kittiwake feathers and barbed with glossy black flint. And there was another weapon: three rawhide thongs an arm's length long, knotted together at one end and weighted at the other with small slices of bone. 'These are slingstones. You know how to use them?'

'I think so, my friend Dark showed me how.'

'Wear them round your waist and tie them with a slip-knot: one tug and you're ready to throw.'

'Why are you telling me this?' said Torak.

'Waste of gear if I don't.' He paused. 'Your wolf…'

'He's not "my" wolf, he's my pack-brother.'

'What's that?'

'Like a friend, but closer.'

Orvo looked puzzled. 'Stay watchful on the fells,' he muttered. 'In summer brown bears roam the hills eating mushrooms and berries. Never camp on the shore, ice bears hunt for carcasses thrown up by the Sea. And don't camp by a noisy stream or you won't hear a bear coming.'

Torak made a face. 'That doesn't leave much.'

The ice river creaked and groaned. Torak heard ice demons booming and hammering to get out. He steered well clear of it, but its freezing breath rocked the skinboat.

Wolf sat tensely in front of him. He hated being back in a boat, but he couldn't have followed on land. Only a bird could have crossed this vast, chaotic river of ice.

A cold day, although thanks to the White Foxes, Torak hardly felt it. If it rained he could wear his seal-hide parka and leggings with the fur on the outside to repel the wet; if it was cold he could wear them with the fur against his skin. He also had a fawn-skin jerkin, warm musk-ox wool socks and thigh-high boots of bearded sealhide with tough flipper-skin feet lined with moss. His salmon-skin gauntlets were strung on reindeer tendons so he couldn't lose them, and a pouch at his waist held a spare pair of salmon-skin socks, and spiked bone bars to strap to his feet for walking on ice: Tanugeak called them 'raven claws'.

The White Foxes' gifts far exceeded the value of the earthblood they'd accepted in return. A waterproof sleeping-sack of seal fur, lined with eider duck skins with the feathers left on; a scrap of reindeer fur to sit on in the boat; and best of all, an eyeshield of polished antler with a notch for the bridge of his nose so that it fitted his face. The eye-slits were as narrow as knife-cuts: as well as shielding him from the glare, they sharpened his sight.

Tanugeak's final gift was a spare knife carved like a lemming gripping the flint blade in its paws. Torak had tied it to his calf under his leggings. Renn did that too, it made him feel closer to her.

Thinking of that now, he felt angry and humiliated. Did she miss him as much as he missed her? Did she? Maybe Inuktiluk was right, and she was better off with Naiginn. But why was she with him at all?

Until now, Torak had never been jealous. He'd had no reason to be. Even when Renn had secrets from him, he'd always known he could count on her.

And I can now, he told himself firmly.

That didn't prevent the fierce heat beating in his blood.

He passed a mountain he remembered: three black peaks rising from a snowfield, like ravens on an ice floe. Somewhere up there was a cave, the Eye of the Viper. Three winters ago he'd been lucky to get out alive.

This was the furthest north he'd ever been. Not even Inuktiluk had ventured beyond the Three Peaks. Few clans did, except for the Narwals.

Wolf was scratching his flanks again. Torak crumbled a little bloodstone and rubbed it in his pack-brother's fur, making them both sneeze. Wolf stopped scratching, but he was still miserable. *Can't we go ashore?*

The weather closed in, Sea and sky melting to grey obscurity dotted with islands. Which way to go?

It flashed across Torak's mind that he could spirit walk in a bird and find out. But spirit walking was dangerous. He never knew the strength of a creature's souls until he was inside them, and while his name-soul and clan-soul became bird, his body would lie unconscious and vulnerable, only his world-soul keeping it alive. Also, flying would anger the north wind. Torak had told it he would never fly again.

Debating what to do, he paddled into a bay tucked behind a headland. Wolf splashed into the shallows and made for a stream while Torak hauled the skinboat onto the shingle.

A snow owl perched on a rock above the shore. Its yellow eyes were ringed with black and it glared a warning like an angry ghost.

Torak licked his lips. 'All right,' he called to the guardian of the Far North. 'I won't spirit walk. I'll fill my waterskin and leave.'

The owl spread its wings and glided away on the wind.

Wolf was running up and down by the stream, sniffing. It took Torak no time at all to spot the tracks. A man's booted feet – Torak could tell he was young because the toe-prints were deeper than the heels – and beside them the smaller, lighter bootprints of a girl.

They were Renn's. Some people fling out their feet like a duck, others turn their feet inwards like a crow. Renn walked in a straight line, like a wolf.

The tracks were fresh. Torak followed them to a boggy patch where she'd picked cloudberries. Cloudberries were her favourites; it was a joke between them that she never left any for him. She'd stripped these bushes bare, except for a single dark-amber berry. Torak put it in his mouth. Burnt-honey sweetness exploded on his tongue.

Wolf stood facing the wind. His tail was taut, his head tilted: he'd smelt something other than prey. He glanced at Torak, then back to the headland.

Waves crashed against it and beyond it rose a drift of windblown smoke.

NINE

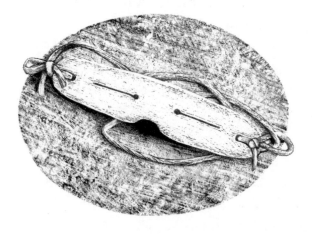

Wolf was *angry*. Because of the pack-sister he'd had to leave his mate and cubs and follow Tall Tailless over these treeless lands where the prey saw him coming from many lopes away. He'd been stuck in that horrible floating hide with nothing to do but be sick, while the Great Wet heaved and murmured and the giant fish yowled in the deeps.

And now at the bottom of the hill the pack-sister was calmly kneeling by a Bright Beast-that-Bites-Hot. She looked and smelt different and she wasn't alone. Crouching beside her was a young male tailless: a smiling pale-pelted stranger. *What did this mean?* Wolf raced back to tell Tall Tailless.

He didn't need to. Tall Tailless had also climbed the hill. His eyes were hard and his face had gone stiff. Wolf knew

he was chewed up inside with love and jealousy and anger
and hurt.

The pack-sister had seen them. So had the unknown
tailless. Slowly they rose to their feet and watched Tall
Tailless walk down the hill towards them.

Wolf followed at a wary distance. He could feel the
tension crackling in his fur. With taillesses as with wolves,
two males and one female meant only one thing: a fight.

'I'll leave you two alone,' said the Narwal boy, backing away
with a rueful smile.

'Thanks, Naiginn,' Renn said without taking her eyes
from Torak.

Torak took off his eyeshield and stared coldly at the boy.

His smile faded. Shaking his head, he raised both hands:
I don't want a quarrel.

We'll see about that, thought Torak.

The White Foxes hadn't warned him that Naiginn was
handsome. And they were right, he looked nothing like a
Narwal. Long fair hair, light-blue eyes, regular features;
the beginnings of a beard limning his jaw with gold. Torak
hated him on sight.

In silence he watched Naiginn trudge across the fells.
When the boy was out of earshot, he turned to Renn.

She stood on the other side of the fire so that he saw
her through a shimmering haze. Ever since she'd left, he'd

imagined what he would say when he found her. But now...
She didn't even look like Renn. That short hair, tendrils caressing her neck like little black snakes. Her eyes looked black too, though they were really dark-brown. Maybe that was because her skin was white from the ash she'd used to hide her clan-tattoos.

The ash had obliterated her freckles, including the one at the corner of her mouth that he particularly liked. This enraged him more than anything. He wanted to shake her and kiss her and yell at her all at once. And she just stood there, huge-eyed, keeping the fire between them.

At last he found his voice. 'Tanugeak told me you'd dyed your hair. If you painted your mouth black you'd look like your mother.'

She flinched. 'I know you're angry with me,' she said in a low voice.

He snorted.

'How did you find me?'

'What does that matter?'

Wolf stood some distance away, watchful and on edge. Renn asked Torak if Darkfur and the cubs had come too.

'Of course not, the cubs are too young. Because of you, Wolf had to leave them behind. You broke up the pack.' He paced up and down, clenching and unclenching his fists. 'Can you imagine what that did to him?'

Her chin went up. 'I did what I had to.'

'Have you any idea what it's been like?'

'Torak—'

'Having to ask strangers if they'd seen you? Having to track you as if you were prey?'

'I couldn't have stayed. I couldn't risk hurting you—'

'You could have *told* me!'

'No, I couldn't. I left so that I wouldn't hurt you. Didn't Dark tell you?'

'You couldn't have hurt me more than you did when you left.'

'Yes, I could, I nearly shot you in the head! What if next time I'd killed you?'

'That was an accident!'

'And the other times? Trust me, Torak, I wouldn't have left if I hadn't been convinced—'

'*Trust* you?' he shouted. 'How can I trust you after this?'

Wolf set back his ears and glanced from one to the other.

'If *I* had been in danger,' Renn said steadily. 'If leaving me had been the only way to keep me safe, you would have done it in a heartbeat. You know you would!'

She was right, but he wouldn't admit it. Why are we fighting? he thought suddenly. I love her and she loves me, that's all that matters. Then he saw Naiginn on the fell and his anger surged back. 'So how does he fit in?' he said savagely.

Renn hesitated, which made him even angrier. 'I didn't believe it when they told me. You with some stranger? It didn't make sense!'

'I met him by chance, I'd got into a riptide and—'

'And *he* just *happened* along?'

'You are so completely on the wrong track it's almost funny. You've no reason to be jealous. Naiginn *helped* me—'

'Oh, I'm sure he did!'

'You've no idea how stupid you're going to feel when I tell you.'

'You're the stupid one! Taking up with a Narwal? Don't you know they call women half-men? They have to walk three paces behind and eat maggots, they're not even allowed to *speak* without permission!'

'Naiginn's not like that.'

'He's a Narwal!' roared Torak. 'They're *all* like that!'

Wolf tucked his tail between his legs and fled.

'Have you finished?' Renn's tone was cool, but her shoulders were up to her ears and she was compressing her lips to stop them trembling.

That went through Torak like an arrow. In two paces he'd crossed the distance between them and pulled her into his arms. 'I'm sorry,' he mumbled.

'I'm sorry too,' she said against his chest.

'It's been horrible since you left. And now finding you with him. And looking so different!'

'You look different too. Where'd you get those clothes?'

'White Foxes. What about you?'

'They gave me some. The rest I made ... before I left.'

'Ah, yes, in secret. Behind my back.'

'I hated that! Those awful days wondering what to do. You do know how much I hated it?'

He looked down at her. He noticed she was wearing his

79

headband, the one he thought he'd lost. Had she noticed that he was wearing the wrist-guard she'd given him?

Their eyes met and they exchanged tentative smiles. Reaching up, she pushed a strand of hair from his forehead. With his forefinger he touched the hidden freckle at the corner of her mouth.

Footsteps crunched towards them. They sprang apart.

'Sorry.' Naiginn grinned. 'I came back too soon, I'll go—'

'Yes, go,' snarled Torak.

'No, stay,' said Renn.

'Why should he?' said Torak. 'He'll be wanting to get back to his clan. Won't you, Naiginn? You helped her, but now I'm here so you can go.'

To Torak's intense irritation, Naiginn turned to Renn and said calmly, 'Haven't you told him?'

'Told me what?' said Torak. 'Renn, what's this about?'

She looked at him. 'You're not going to believe this. At first I didn't believe it myself. But Naiginn told me so many things that he couldn't possibly have known—'

'Believe *what*?' cried Torak.

Renn glanced at Naiginn, then back to Torak. She took a breath. 'He's my brother.'

TEN

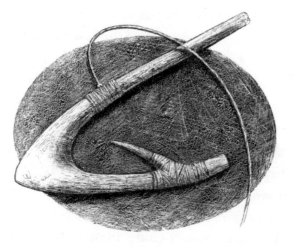

'I know you don't believe me but it's true,' said Renn. 'Naiginn is my brother. His mother was the Viper Mage.'

'So why'd you never mention him before?' said Torak.

'I didn't know he existed! I thought it was just me and Hord. It never occurred to me there was anyone else.'

'Because there ISN'T!' yelled Torak. 'He made up the whole thing!'

'Why would I do that?' Naiginn said reasonably.

'How should I know?' retorted Torak.

'Torak, listen to yourself!' snapped Renn. 'Do you really think I'm so easily fooled?'

'I'm beginning to wonder.'

Flinging up her arms, she stalked off. Then she marched back. 'Just hear what he has to say, will you?'

Torak folded his arms on his chest.

'I understand why you're suspicious,' said Naiginn. 'But it's true, the Viper Mage was my mother.' He squatted to feed driftwood to the fire. 'One summer my father was on the fells when he saw a woman walking towards him out of a blaze of sunlight. She said her name was Ankanau. She said she came from the sun.'

He paused, watching the flames. 'She stayed with him for two summers. She had me. Then she left. My father waited but she didn't come back. He stared at the sun for so long he went blind. I've hated the sun ever since.' He fed another stick to the fire. 'In our clan if a man can't hunt, we strangle him. They didn't strangle my father because he's our Mage. It would have been better if they had. She broke his heart. When Renn told me she was dead, I was glad.'

'Sounds like her, doesn't it?' Renn said bitterly.

'Lots of women leave their mates,' Torak flung back.

'And their children?' Naiginn said in a hard voice. 'Because of her I always felt separate. Like my sister.'

'Half-sister,' muttered Torak. '*If* that.'

'Oh, Torak!' cried Renn.

'No, he's right,' said Naiginn. 'You and I had different fathers, which makes us half-brother and -sister. But we're still bone kin.'

Torak set his teeth.

'It's true,' insisted Renn. 'He described our mother *exactly*, including her clan-tattoos, and he's never even *seen* a viper!'

'If she left when he was a baby, how could he know what she looked like?'

'Because she came back,' said Naiginn. 'I was seven. She stayed for two summers, as she had before. When winter came and ice conquered the Sea, she left – this time for ever. She broke my father's heart all over again.'

Despite himself, Torak could see a resemblance between Naiginn and Renn: the same high-boned features. But Renn's face was alive with her thoughts and feelings, like sunlight on fast water – while Naiginn's had a curious immobility, even when he smiled; and he rarely blinked.

Torak realized they were watching him. 'All right,' he said. 'Suppose – just *suppose* – he is your half-brother. What difference does it make? He's nothing to do with why you came north.'

'Yes, he is. Tell him, Naiginn.'

The Narwal boy rose. 'A while ago my father, Marupai, had a dream. He dreamt all the prey disappeared and our people were starving. Then a raven flew up from the south. It had a broken wing, my father healed it, and in return the raven brought back the prey and our people were saved. My father sent me south to find the raven.' He paused. 'When I first met Renn I thought she was a Sea-eagle. Then the spray washed the ash from her cheek and I saw her clan-tattoo.' He smiled. 'I knew I'd found my raven.'

'She's not *your* raven,' growled Torak.

'Torak, believe me, I was as astonished as Renn when we found out we were kin! But surely now you understand?

83

Only Renn can help my clan, and only Marupai can help *her*! If anyone can solve the riddle, he can. He can put an end to whatever is endangering your life!'

Torak glanced from Naiginn to Renn, then back to Naiginn. He shook his head. 'You're asking me to believe that out of all the hunters in the Far North she just *happens* to come across you? And you just *happen* to be the half-brother she never knew she had? And your father just *happens* to be the only man who can help her?' He turned to Renn. 'You actually believe this?'

'Yes, I do.'

'Because it's true!' cried Naiginn. 'Renn and I were *meant* to find each other! And whether you believe it or not, Torak, believe this: I *will* save my clan. I *will* take her north to our settlement at Waigo and I *will* take her to Marupai!'

'Don't you mind when he talks about "taking" you north, as if you were a spare paddle?' Torak asked Renn.

'He doesn't mean it like that.'

'Yes, he does, Narwals treat women as if they're things.'

'As far as you're concerned, whatever he says is wrong.'

He didn't reply.

She and Naiginn had pitched camp in a sheltered hollow, and Torak had fetched his boat from behind the headland and turned it into a shelter for him and Renn. At the clan meet she'd traded the deerhide canoe for a skinboat, a smaller one, which Torak had placed on the other side of the fire to throw back the heat as they slept. He was piling rocks around it to make a wall that would cut them off from Naiginn, who'd left his own boat on the shore and tactfully carried his sleeping-sack some distance upstream.

'Why won't you even listen to him?' Renn said crossly as she baited fishing-hooks with whelks.

'Either he's your half-brother, or he's lying about everything. There is no in-between.'

'You're not giving him a chance. And stop needling him!'

'I'm not.'

'Yes, you are. Just now when he helped carry your boat, you stood next to him so that he had to look up to you, because you're taller.'

Torak chuckled. 'He didn't like that. I think he's vain.'

'Sh! He's coming!'

'I'm going fishing,' called Naiginn. 'I'll leave you two to talk things over.'

'Good,' Torak called back.

'Go with him,' said Renn. 'You need to get to know each other.'

'No, we don't,' said Torak.

'That's fine,' said Naiginn with a rueful grin. 'Besides, I'm going after halibut—'

'Meaning what?' said Torak.

'Well, you don't know how to catch them. And they're really dangerous.'

'What, like walruses?' mocked Torak.

'No,' Naiginn said patiently. 'But they're strong and they fight hard.'

He spoke with no hint of a challenge, and yet Torak bristled. 'Changed my mind. I'll come and lend a hand.'

Naiginn shrugged, and Renn threw Torak a look: *Try to get along!*

Out of respect for the Sea Mother, the two boys tied back their hair and made sure their clothes were clean, then washed in the shallows and rubbed their faces and hands with seaweed to take away their scent. Naiginn took much longer than Torak, he wasn't satisfied till his clothes were spotless. He wore a beautifully made parka and leggings of bleached gutskin painted with black stripes, and seal-hide boots fringed at the tops. His weapons had to be spotless too: barbed bone harpoon, axe, knife, bow, arrows of gleaming black flint. 'Don't touch,' he warned Torak. 'Some of them are poisoned.'

'I'm not a child,' said Torak.

Naiginn's fishing gear was a very long coil of tough twisted kelp and a hook of a kind Torak hadn't seen before. Bigger than his hand, it was a piece of forked driftwood with an inward-pointing bone barb tied to one fork with sinew. Naiginn had already baited it with a chunk of octopus he'd caught on the rocks.

'It works like this,' he explained, to Torak's irritation. 'The fish sucks in the bait, can't swallow it and tries to spit it out. That's when the barb snags its cheek. The trick is to make the size of the hook just right: you want to catch a halibut big enough to get its mouth around the whole hook, but not so big that it'll flip the boat.'

Torak thought of the man-sized fish at the clan meet with both eyes on the same side of its face. 'Are halibut really that strong?'

'Oh, many a hunter's gone after them and never come back.'

Torak met the pale-blue gaze and wondered if Naiginn was trying to scare him. 'Why's the line so long?'

'Halibut feed on the Sea bottom. That's why you need a big sink-stone, to take the hook all the way down. I tie the line around it with a special knot, so it'll come loose at a tug and the sink-stone will stay on the bottom: that way we only have to haul up the fish.' He studied Torak. 'It'll take both of us to bring one in. And be careful not to get snagged in the line—'

'I have been fishing before, you know.'

'Not for halibut. They fight hard, Torak. That's what this is for.' He held up a driftwood club. 'Soon as we get the fish near the boat, we kill it. Can't risk hauling it in till it's dead, or it'll smash us to pieces.'

'Right,' said Torak.

He wasn't frightened, but he was uncomfortably aware that he was about to give Naiginn a splendid opportunity to make a fool of him.

ELEVEN

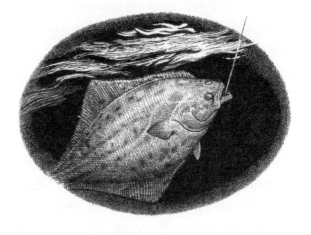

Naiginn cast the fishing gear over the side of the boat and he and Torak settled down to wait. Between them the end of the line lay coiled like a greenish-brown snake. Bobbing on the waves and tied to the line was a seal-stomach float: if it went under, they'd know they'd hooked a fish.

Naiginn tossed Torak a flat piece of driftwood. 'Be ready to wind the line round that as soon as I start drawing it in. Don't be tempted to wind it round your hand or you'll get pulled overboard.'

Torak threw him a look.

It was warm in the sun. They'd left their outer clothing onshore and sat barefoot in jerkins and under-leggings. The wind was rampaging elsewhere and the Sea was calm.

They weren't far from the coast, as Naiginn said halibut liked to feed in river mouths. Torak watched Renn casting her hooks from the rocks.

'Back at camp,' said Naiginn, 'I noticed you've painted your baler red. Why's that?'

'Trick I learnt from a Seal Clan boy,' said Torak without turning his head. 'Makes it easier to spot if you drop it overboard.'

'Clever. I'll try it.'

Stop trying to make friends, Torak thought sourly.

Then he relented and took his medicine horn from his pouch. 'I've got earthblood. If you've got seal oil we could do it now.'

Smiling, Naiginn shook his head. 'That horn looks like red deer antler. We don't mix Forest and Sea.'

'Ah, I forgot.' He frowned. 'How did you know it's red deer if you've never been to the Forest?'

'Because I have. When I was younger my father sent me to learn the ways of the Far South. I was fostered with the Swans in the Mountains and the Aurochs in the Deep Forest. The same old man who made Renn's bow made one for me.'

'Then you must have seen a viper. You told her you hadn't.'

'It's the truth, Torak. I was in the Forest in spring-time, the vipers hadn't woken up.'

Torak grunted.

'I saw lots of other creatures, though. So much *life*, I

couldn't believe it! All those teeming souls… The hunting was much easier than what I'm used to.'

'What do you mean?'

'Prey doesn't leave tracks in the Sea.'

'Tracking's not as easy as you think.'

'I didn't say it was.' He rearranged his grip on the line. 'Renn says you're the best tracker in the Forest. She says you could track a ghost over solid rock.'

Torak didn't reply. He wondered what else Renn had said about him.

The sun climbed higher and he watched the play of waterlight through the skinboat's translucent sides.

'That's my first memory,' said Naiginn. 'Watching the waves through my uncle's boat. In our clan boys aren't raised by their fathers but by their uncles.'

'I know,' said Torak. 'Fathers aren't harsh enough and you have to grow up tough. Unlike us Softbellies.'

'I meant that I envy you,' Naiginn said quietly. 'I'm only one summer younger than you and Renn, but I look older. People in my clan age fast. I had no idea that living could be fun until I went south.'

His tone was matter-of-fact, and Torak repressed a twinge of pity.

'You don't believe I'm her brother,' said Naiginn.

'No, but she does. That's what counts.'

Naiginn sighed. 'Believe me, the last thing I want is to come between you.'

'Then give up any idea of "taking" her north.'

'I can't! But, Torak, know this: whatever happens, I will help you in any way I can.' He spoke with peculiar urgency, as if with some hidden message.

'The only way you can help,' said Torak, 'is to forget about—'

The float went under with a plop. Naiginn yanked the line. 'We've got a bite.'

He drew in the line a few lengths, then let it out again, repeating this several times so that the fish would tire itself. 'It's big,' he muttered. Torak knew that already. The boat was rocking, he had to lean back to steady it.

Hauling in the line was slow, grinding work. Naiginn's face grew red, the tendons on his neck bulged. Twice his grip slipped. Torak offered to take over but he refused.

Some time later, he agreed. 'Make sure you keep the line taut,' he gasped, 'or it'll steal the bait.'

'I know,' growled Torak.

As he took the line he felt the power of the monster fish cutting into his palms. Hand over painful hand, he dragged it closer. The fish was cunning, letting the line go slack, then putting on a burst of speed and trying to dive under the boat. Torak was soaked in sweat, his arms trembling with strain.

At last he glimpsed a huge pale-green form thrashing and twisting underwater. 'It's coming,' he muttered.

With a drenching splash the fish broke the surface, nearly flipping the boat. 'The club!' shouted Naiginn. 'It's behind you, I can't reach—'

As Torak groped for the club his grip on the line briefly slackened. The fish seized its chance and dived. Flinging himself backwards, Torak hauled with all his might. Naiginn had thrown down the driftwood and was snatching at the line. Torak cried out as his leg was yanked from under him: the line was twisted round his calf. He grabbed the side of the boat but the halibut was strong, it was dragging him overboard.

Suddenly the pull on his leg went slack and he fell into the boat. Naiginn had cut the line.

Mocking waves slapped the sides as Torak pushed himself upright. Blood was dripping from a gash in his calf. He felt horribly foolish.

'I told you to stay clear of the line!' shouted Naiginn.

'I thought I had!'

'Well, it's gone now! Your leg: are you all right?'

'I'm fine.'

'It's bleeding.'

'I said I'm fine!'

In strained silence they took up their paddles and headed for the beach.

Renn blenched when she saw Torak limping ashore. 'Now do you understand why I left?'

'How could it be your fault?' he said. 'You weren't even there.'

'The very *day* that you find me and you nearly drown!'

'It was *my fault*, I should've kept clear of the line.' He was furious and embarrassed: he'd nearly been pulled overboard by a fish. And there was no convincing Renn that it was an accident.

Naiginn had stayed by his boat to make another halibut hook. Torak and Renn trudged without speaking to their camp, where Renn took her finest bone needle and sinew thread and sewed up his wound.

'Sorry,' she muttered as she dug in her needle.

'Doesn't hurt,' he lied.

When she'd finished she took a little birch-bark box from her medicine pouch and smeared the wound with pine-pitch.

'I've missed that smell,' he said.

'Me too.' She put her hand on his knee. 'I miss trees and hazelnuts and roast boar.'

'Stewed elk and lingonberries.'

They looked at each other.

'Most of all I've missed you,' said Torak.

Rip and Rek flew past making cuckoo calls, then disappeared over the fells.

'Why do they keep doing that?' said Torak.

'I don't know,' said Renn, scratching the scar on her hand. Torak told her about the scar on his forearm itching, and how Wolf kept scratching his flanks. 'What d'you think is causing it? I'm pretty sure it's not midges or fleas.'

'I've been wondering if it's my Soul-Eater marrow,' she said. 'You have that too. And Wolf has eaten Soul-Eater flesh.'

'But why hasn't it happened before?'

'I don't know. All I have is questions. No answers.'

She looked unhappy. Torak took her hands in his. 'Tanugeak told me about the riddle. We can solve it. Together.'

'No, Torak, no! As long as you're with me you're in danger!'

'You can't seriously think I'll go back to the Forest without you?'

'But don't you see, nothing's changed! I couldn't bear it if anything happened to you!'

They were still miserably arguing when Naiginn joined them and it was time to eat.

While he and Torak had been failing to catch halibut, Renn had caught three rockfish from the shore. She'd baked two in seaweed and stewed a pile of roseroot from the fell. Torak noticed that she left most of her fish as an offering and gave him all the roseroot.

Naiginn ate his fish raw, sucking the brains and saving the eyes and tongue till last. 'We prefer our food raw or rotten,' he said with a grin. 'I never liked Forest food. All that greenstuff!'

'Seaweed's green too,' said Torak. 'So's roseroot.'

'Which is why I don't eat it,' said Naiginn. Soon afterwards he went upstream to his camp, leaving Torak and Renn alone.

They lay side by side in separate sleeping-sacks. Torak was annoyed to find that he could hardly keep his eyes open.

'You might *try* to get along with him,' Renn said crossly.

'He's too eager to please and he smiles too much, but it doesn't mean anything. And he spent ages cleaning his clothes.'

'That's out of respect for the Sea Mother.'

'Rip and Rek don't like him, they haven't come near us. Neither has Wolf.'

'Rip and Rek are moulting, it makes them sulky. Besides, you know it takes them ages to get used to strangers. Same for Wolf.'

Torak rolled on his side to face her. 'Naiginn's got an odd walk, have you noticed? Sort of stiff, as if he's still learning. And his left foot turns out, like a duck.'

Scowling, she curled up with her back to him. 'Well, like him or not, he's my bone kin, so you'd better learn to get along.'

Torak had no intention of getting along with Naiginn, but he was too sleepy to reply.

Hail woke him hammering on the skinboat. Renn was not beside him.

He scrambled out of the shelter. The fire was dead. Renn's skinboat was gone. He ran down to the shore. Naiginn's boat was gone too.

Wolf raced up to him, panting an apology for not waking him: he'd tried, but his pack-brother had been fast asleep.

'Renn!' shouted Torak. The icy wind tore her name from his lips.

He felt fogged and unsteady. He remembered Renn offering him roseroot but eating none herself. Oh, Renn. He wondered what she'd put in it to make him sleep.

And she'd done something else to slow him down: she'd taken his provisions. The salmon cakes, the auroch-blood sausage he'd saved from the Forest, the White Foxes' wind-dried whale meat. It was so like her: simple yet devastatingly effective. To survive he would have to hunt and fish, and meanwhile she and Naiginn would be getting further and further ahead.

He wasn't angry with her, he was angry with himself. 'Nothing's changed,' she'd told him. And he'd been too intent on hating Naiginn to notice. So she'd done the only thing she could do. She'd left him again.

TWELVE

What have I done? Renn thought bleakly.

She pictured Torak waking and finding her gone. She remembered how he'd looked when he'd found her with Naiginn. His face had been inscrutable as he'd made his way towards them, his eyeshield of slitted bone emphasizing the clean-cut severity of his mouth. He would never forgive her for leaving him a second time.

The strange thing was that she'd known she was making a terrible mistake even as she was drugging the roseroot, and waking Naiginn and stealing away. It was all wrong but she'd done it anyway. She'd felt as if she was outside herself, watching someone else.

'I can't believe you took his food.' Naiginn had slowed and was paddling beside her, shaking his head in admiration.

'I had to,' she muttered. 'Making him hunt is the only way to slow him down.'

'Oh, there's no chance of him finding us now.'

'You don't know Torak. He won't give up. And he has Wolf.'

'What difference does that make?'

'Wolf's nose is so keen he could find me in a blizzard.'

'Trust me, they'll never catch us.' Naiginn moved ahead.

Soon afterwards he swerved out to Sea. 'Whales feeding! Keep well clear!'

For a while Renn forgot about Torak. The Sea was churning, the boats leaping like hares in spring-time. Kittiwakes were screaming and diving after their share as the whales slammed the Sea with enormous tails to stun their prey, flinging themselves sideways, flailing immensely long flippers and baring huge pleated bellies before crashing down with throaty pffs! of spray.

Even after they'd left the whales behind, Naiginn remained in front. Renn had noticed that he didn't like it if she took the lead.

If Torak was here, she thought, we'd take turns in front. We'd have a race and he'd win. I'd splash him and we'd end up drenching each other and laughing... What am I *doing*, paddling after a half-brother I hardly know?

Before her in the boat lay Tanugeak's parting gift: a small hollowed-out sealskin with a drawstring at the neck which turned it into a neat, waterproof pack. Tanugeak had done a cleansing charm on Renn's bow to appease the Sea Mother, and given her a gutskin quiver and arrows of light, strong whale bone. Renn was grateful, but now it struck her that with all this new gear, and her seal-hide clothes and walrus-hide boat, she had almost nothing left from the Forest.

No wonder Wolf hadn't come near her. She had broken up the pack. With a jolt of terror, she wondered if she would ever find her way back.

'There's a spring in that bay,' called Naiginn. 'We'll go ashore and fill our waterskins.'

Renn didn't like the bay. It had a feeling of violence and catastrophe. The faces of the cliffs were slashed as if by a giant axe, and steam floated over the spring, which had the rotten-egg smell of bloodstone. Dipping in her hand, she recoiled with a cry: the water was *hot*.

'The earth's hide is thinner here,' said Naiginn in an undertone. 'The Otherworld is very close.'

'I can feel it. Demons fighting to get out.'

He looked surprised. 'I can't feel anything. Must be your Mage's sense.'

She didn't reply.

He said, 'If you're worried about Torak catching up, why don't you do a charm to throw that wolf off the scent?'

'I don't want to.'

'Why not?'

'Couldn't you do one instead? Both your parents were Mages, you must be better at it than me.'

He shook his head. 'I'm merely a hunter, no skill at

Magecraft.' From his voice she could tell that he disliked admitting it.

On the wind she caught a clamour and a whiff of bird droppings. She followed Naiginn round a spur, into an echoing din.

Towering cliffs rang with the wails of thousands of seabirds. Raucous clans of guillemots and kittiwakes fought for space as they guarded their chicks from mean-eyed skuas on the lookout for an easy meal. The cliffs were white with droppings, the wind gusting a throat-catching stink.

A kittiwake smacked into the Sea near Naiginn, emerging with a beakful of wriggling capelin. A skua bullied the smaller bird into sicking up its catch, then swallowed it in mid-air. Naiginn laughed.

A puffin flew past Renn and crashed into the water in front of her boat. The puffin's beak was stuffed with fish and it was so laden it couldn't take off. Desperate to get out of her way, it rowed its stubby wings and paddled its broad orange feet. Renn swerved. At last the bird lumbered into the air and flew back to a puffin-sized cave where its chicks were waiting.

Rip and Rek were swooping at a row of guillemots huddled on a ledge. The guillemots flung themselves into the air with weird groaning cries and both ravens flew off holding eggs in their beaks. They spattered the Sea with droppings. This gave Renn an idea. 'I think I know how to put Wolf off the scent!' she shouted to Naiginn.

'Don't go too close,' he shouted back. 'The cliffs are restless, if you annoy them they'll fling rocks!'

She swerved just in time to avoid hitting a submerged rock.

'Turn back, you're too close!' yelled Naiginn.

'I need the droppings!' But she knew this wasn't only about putting Wolf off the scent, it was about punishing herself for leaving Torak.

As she paddled into the chill shadow of the cliffs, the clamour of birds became deafening and the stench made her blink. The Sea was a strange vivid turquoise, littered with white feathers. A dead kittiwake rocked on the waves, staring at her with lifeless eyes. Glancing up, she was instantly dizzy. Seabirds speckled the sky like grey snow. Fin-Kedinn had told her once that there were always as many birds *under* the waves as you could see above – and it was true: beneath the skinboat she glimpsed seabirds flitting through the water like pallid ghosts.

'Renn, turn back! I mean it!' Naiginn sounded cross.

The smell was so bad she had to breathe through her mouth. Pebbles were raining down. The cliffs didn't like her being so close.

The swell lifted the boat and slapped it against a rock. Yanking off her gauntlet, she scraped her hand across it. It came away sticky and white. Gagging at the stench, she rubbed the slime on her parka. Good. Do it again.

'Come back *at once!*' Naiginn was furious.

The cliffs were hurling bigger stones, one striking her

painfully on the shoulder. Grimly she went on plastering her parka with filth. When she was smeared and stinking, she pushed off with her paddle and headed out to Sea.

'What were you *doing*? You could've been killed!' Naiginn's handsome face was swollen with rage.

'I had to throw Wolf off the scent.'

'I *told* you to come back!'

'So what?'

They glared at each other.

Naiginn shook himself. 'You're mad, you know that? And you stink.'

She gave him a lopsided grin. 'That's the idea.'

He grunted. 'Promise that when we pitch camp you'll stay downwind.'

'Promise.' She felt a bit better. She'd found a way to throw Wolf off the scent that didn't involve Magecraft – and it was nothing like what her mother would have done.

Then it hit her that Torak and Wolf would never find her now, and a void opened up inside and she wanted to howl.

THIRTEEN

The ice bear's tracks shouted at Torak from the shore. Each paw-print was twice the size of his head: very fresh and very deep. The bear that had made these tracks was enormous.

Slowly Torak rose to his feet. The charcoal sand was littered with silver driftwood and bleached bones. The cliffs at the far end of the bay had collapsed in a jumble of dark-pink granite. At this end he caught the rotten-egg smell of the stream. Like the previous stream it would be hot and taste nasty, but he was too thirsty to care. Or he had been until he'd seen the tracks.

The ice bear had ambled the length of the shore with her cubs, seeking carcasses to scavenge. Torak couldn't tell if she'd walked into the Sea, or onto the fells.

He couldn't *see* the fells. Above the beach the Sea had eaten away the black rocks to make a man-high ridge that hid them from view.

Ice bears are great wanderers. Torak pictured the massive female he'd encountered before the clan meet. She could be hunkered down behind that ridge right now, watching him. He wouldn't know until it was too late.

Wolf appeared on the ridge, panting and wagging his tail. Tension poured out of Torak. If an ice bear was near, Wolf would know.

Having filled his waterskin, he stowed it in the boat and turned his attention to finding something to eat. He'd been in such haste to catch up with Renn that he'd passed the bird cliffs without shooting a single guillemot, and when he'd seen the whales dozing on the surface after their meal he hadn't stopped to scoop up their leavings. He regretted that now, he hadn't eaten for nearly two days. Renn's trick of stealing his provisions was proving ruthlessly effective. And more worryingly, Wolf had lost her scent. Torak suspected she'd done something to mask it.

Plenty of fish in the shallows, so he baited his hooks with water-snails and cast them off the rocks, then climbed onto the fells to hunt.

Windswept wastes pocked with shivering lakes and patches of snow. Beyond them, fog-wreathed mountains under a heavy slate sky.

A hare darted off. Torak's arrow just missed.

Wolf was slinking towards a patch of snow on the other side of a lake. Torak dropped to the ground. That wasn't snow, it was a flock of geese. They were snow geese: white, with scarlet beaks and feet – and after grazing all summer, mouth-wateringly plump.

Torak belly-crawled closer while they waddled and pecked, squabbling as they kept watch over their fat grey goslings.

This wasn't going to be as easy as he'd thought. The ground was littered with feathers and down, but the geese had finished moulting and their goslings were big enough to fly.

He was taking aim when the flock rose in a honking cloud, black wingtips flashing. He missed. Already they were out of range, a white arrow speeding with high wild cries over the wolf-grey Sea.

The wind hissed mockingly. A fox in its dark summer pelt trotted by with a gosling in its jaws and cast Torak a scornful glance. *Didn't you get one?*

Torak gathered a few mouse-nibbled mushrooms and frost-blackened crowberries. He found a dead wolverine frozen in mid-snarl. He wasn't quite hungry enough for that – although not far off.

A pair of diverbirds had settled on the lake. An easy target, a child of five could hit one.

Not Torak. The diverbirds flew away with shivering cries.

Something was wrong. He'd heard of people losing their

hunting luck but it had never happened to him. With a sigh he went to check his fishing lines.

As he followed the creek back to the shore, he came on the remains of a dead ice bear. It was horribly thin. Had it died of starvation? If the best hunter in the Far North couldn't catch enough prey, what hope for him?

He noticed two odd-looking puncture wounds in the bear's sunken flank. They were a handspan apart and deep, as if a two-pronged spear had pierced its side. Torak had never heard of any clan hunting ice bears.

His fishing lines came up empty – and yet he could *see* fish in the shallows. Maybe there were mussels on the rocks. The icy water numbed his fingers as he pulled up slimy handfuls of seaweed – but no mussels, not even a whelk. And it wasn't the kind of seaweed he could eat.

The snow owl perched on the rise, glaring with fierce yellow eyes. At last Torak understood. Tanugeak had told him the guardian of the Far North didn't want him here and she was right. This owl knew that he'd killed one of its kin. To punish him it had taken his hunting luck.

'It wasn't my fault!' he called. 'They made me do it!'

As he got to his feet, spots swam before his eyes and he nearly pitched forwards. When he looked again, the owl was gone.

And now at the far end of the shore the rockfall was coming alive. A mountain of dark-pink blubber was bellowing and lumbering towards him.

The walruses moved at appalling speed, thrusting at the

sand with great yellow tusks, hauling themselves forwards on ungainly flippers. Suddenly Torak knew what had killed that ice bear.

And they were coming right at him.

FOURTEEN

No time to reach the boat, the walruses would cut him off. Torak turned and fled for the ridge.

The rocks were slippery, he couldn't find a way up. Over his shoulder he saw a huge bull walrus leave the herd and come after him. Its juddering bulk was covered in warts, its tusks as long as his arm. As he clawed for a handhold he saw lice seething in its creviced flesh, he caught the rank stink of rage. Its hot little eyes grazed his but it wasn't after him, it was glaring at something above.

The ice bear leapt over Torak and attacked a smaller walrus. The bull lashed out with its tusks. The bear dodged, the tusks splintering rock near Torak's head. He was as threatening as a shrimp to the walrus, but if he got in its way it would flatten him and not even notice.

Now the ice bear was at the rear of the herd, trying to pick off a baby walrus. The bear struck, but the calf's hide was so thick the great claws didn't even draw blood. The bull flung round in defence of its young. Torak seized his chance and scrambled up the ridge.

No sign of Wolf, still far off on the fells. Too breathless to howl, Torak raced along the ridge. The beach was a heaving mass of blubber, but if he could get to the creek before the walruses, he could skirt round and reach the boat.

Below him the ice bear was snarling and swiping at the bull in clouds of black sand. The bull knew he was winning. Flinging up his head he roared: *This beach is mine! Mine! Mine!* Again he lunged, again the bear withdrew. She was losing ground fast, backing towards the stream. Torak had to reach it first.

As he splashed into its unclean heat he slipped. The walrus charged and the bear sprang back, narrowly missing Torak, who skittered past. With startling suddenness the shore had emptied, nothing between him and the boat – but the bay was boiling with walruses diving, rearing, spouting spray. And still no sign of Wolf.

Torak couldn't wait any longer. Flinging the boat into the shallows, he dug in his paddle, desperately steering between streaming backs and sputtering heads.

When he was out in the bay he howled for his pack-brother.

Where was Wolf?

Pawing the earth with its hoof, the musk-ox swept its massive head from side to side, trying to hook Wolf on its horns. Each time it charged he backed away, then moved in again, keeping nose to nose with his prey so that it couldn't gore his flank.

If his mate had been with him she would have distracted it by biting its rump. To attack alone was too risky. Wolf gave up.

Spotting a female who was limping, he leapt at her back. She was so shaggy his jaws bit nothing but wool, no actual flesh. Spitting out furballs, he jumped down in disgust. The female trotted away and started to graze.

Wolf loped up a hill to catch the scents blowing from the mountains. He smelt that the reindeer were far off in the heights and the white wolves had followed them. He heard rock-squirrels among boulders; but he'd learnt that one always kept watch and squeaked a warning to the others.

Midges engulfed him in a whining cloud. Writhing and snapping, he trotted miserably to a smelly little Fast Wet – but when he lapped, *it bit his tongue.* What kind of Fast Wet bites *hot?*

More and more, Wolf hated these treeless lands where the Great Bright Eye never slept and there were no Darks. He missed his pack terribly, and he was *furious* with the pack-sister. She had left Tall Tailless *again – and she had left with another male.* No she-wolf would ever do this. Tall Tailless should forget her and find a new mate. They should go back to the Forest and rejoin the pack.

The wind turned and Wolf smelt bear. He caught the distant roars of giant fish-dogs, the ones with tusks.

Then faint and far, he heard something that made his pelt tighten with dread: Tall Tailless's desperate howls.

Torak had howled for Wolf till he was hoarse, but still nothing.

A walrus surfaced, soaking him in spray. One slash of her tusks would sink the boat, and judging by her glare, she knew whose hides it was made of. Torak swerved to avoid her. She watched him go, rolled over and disappeared.

At last Torak spotted Wolf hurtling down the beach and into the Sea. For a moment his muzzle showed above the waves – then he vanished in the swell.

Walruses reared as Torak paddled towards where he'd seen his pack-brother. For an age he saw nothing. Then he glimpsed a small wet head in the heaving, grunting herd. Wolf looked tiny and horribly vulnerable. He kept bobbing out of sight.

When Torak finally reached him he was bedraggled and exhausted. Grabbing him under the forelegs, Torak heaved, summoning every last shred of strength to haul him aboard.

The walruses had vanished, taking the wind with them. The sun lay on the Sea, the land loomed dark against the violet sky. The only sounds were waves slapping the boat, and Torak panting.

Wolf shook himself and licked his pack-brother's chin, none the worse for his swim. Torak was shaking and spent.

Suddenly Wolf uttered a deep, shuddering growl.

The ice bear had fetched her cubs from their hiding-place and slipped into the Sea. She was swimming right past the boat. Her ears were flat against her skull, her powerful forepaws thrusting aside the green water. For a moment she turned her head and stared at Torak. Then the swell hid her from view.

He paddled till he was dizzy, his body screaming for rest. He couldn't get the ice bear out of his mind. He'd got a good look at her when she was fighting that walrus. Her belly hung so low it almost brushed the sand – but she wasn't pregnant, she was fat. That she could feed herself and two cubs through the lean times of summer meant she must be an extraordinarily skilful hunter.

The best hunters are those who know how to pick the weakest prey. That was why she'd panicked the walruses, to see which couldn't fight back. That was why she'd stared at Torak. She knew he was weak, and getting weaker.

He would not forget her flat black stare and he knew that she would not forget him. *I am hungry,* that stare had said. *You are prey.*

FIFTEEN

Renn hated skinboating. Seawater made her eyes smart despite her eyeshield, and while Naiginn effortlessly skimmed the waves she bumped along behind, getting splashed.

'I wish you didn't stink,' he grumbled for the tenth time.

'It'll be worth it if it's thrown Wolf off the scent.'

'You could've done that by Magecraft. You have the skill, why not use it? I would.'

'Not if it reminded you of our mother, you wouldn't.'

'Yes, I would.'

They'd been bickering incessantly. At the bird cliffs he'd got slightly spattered and spent ages cleaning his clothes.

At their next camp he'd sulked because she'd shot more geese than him. He reminded her of her older brother Hord: whatever he did, he had to be best.

Torak wasn't like that. He didn't mind that she was a better shot than him. As for her clothes, she could be as messy as she wanted, it wouldn't occur to him to care.

She glanced at Naiginn's handsome profile. Torak was right, he did smile too much. Torak only smiled when he had a reason, and then it was worth waiting for.

He was right about Naiginn's walk too. He didn't swing his arms and he moved awkwardly. *Like he's still learning*, Torak had said with lethal accuracy.

With a pang Renn pictured Torak's loose, vigorous stride. And the little green flecks in his grey eyes, and the way he looked at her in the dappled sunlight of the Forest.

Pushing up the sleeve of her parka, she touched his headband wound round her wrist. It was salt-stained and no longer smelt of him.

Naiginn paddled ahead, then waited for her to catch up. He did that a lot, it was really annoying.

'I'm sorry,' he muttered.

She shot him a glance. 'Me too.'

Now she felt bad. What did it matter if he was vain? It wasn't his fault if he'd grown up in a clan which treated women as half-men. He was still getting used to a girl talking back, or even talking at all.

'You're worried about Torak,' he said quietly.

She nodded.

'He's a hunter, he won't starve.'

It wasn't that. Torak would be furious with her for leaving him again, but underneath he'd be unhappy. Renn knew the way his mind worked. She knew how good he was at blaming himself. 'I know you miss Fin-Kedinn and your clan,' he'd told her once. 'I don't, because I'm clanless, and that's hard for you.'

She'd told him that was ridiculous. But what if he was beginning to wonder if the real reason she'd left was that she no longer wanted to be with him?

Out loud she said, 'I'm getting nowhere. I'm no closer to finding out why I'm a danger to Torak than when I left.'

'We'll be at Waigo soon. My father will know what to do.'

'What about the riddle? I haven't even begun to solve it.'

'Marupai will help.'

Renn did not reply. Somewhere, the spirit of her mother was laughing. She pictured Seshru's beautiful heartless face and her sideways smile. *You're not doing too well, are you, daughter? You've left your mate a second time and hurt him even more.*

The wind dropped, the Sun rested on the waves, and flakes of gold rocked on the quiet Sea as they searched for a campsite. Renn was so tired she would have camped on a rock, but Naiginn was infuriatingly fussy.

'What about there?' She pointed to an inlet.

'The last people who camped there died of fever, no one's been near it since.'

He rejected the next bay because its hot springs stank.

'I don't *care* about the smell,' yawned Renn.

'I do. My people call it the demon breath, we never—'

'Right,' she snapped. 'Let's try that island, shall we?'

'What island?'

She pointed at a dark line on the shining Sea.

'There is no island,' he said flatly.

'You may not like it that my eyes are better than yours—'

'I've known these waters all my life, there is no island!'

'But I can *see* it!'

'Where are you going?'

'To camp on the island!'

From this distance it looked perfect: low-lying, but with no rim of surf to warn of rocks that would make it hard to get ashore. She saw seabirds wheeling above it, and where there are seabirds there are fish.

But as she paddled closer, a whale spout showed white against the land. Another whale blew. And another.

'Better leave it to the whales,' Naiginn called smugly.

Renn didn't reply. There was something odd about the island. It seemed to be rocking on the swell.

Drawing nearer, she saw a dense flock of seabirds rise from its western edge. More birds flew up to join them, forming a dark cloud that wavered and stretched as it veered across the island, then settled at the other end.

'It isn't an island,' Renn said in an altered voice. 'At least – not one where we can camp.'

What she'd taken for land was an immense flock of seabirds floating on the waves. An island made of birds. *To find what you seek, you must put the island of wings to flight.*

'Those whales are hunting!' shouted Naiginn. 'Don't go too close!'

'It's part of the riddle!' she called over her shoulder. 'It's the island of wings, I have to make it fly!'

He yelled something she didn't catch. Paddling closer, she heard the loud rheu! of spouting whales – but she wasn't frightened, she knew they didn't eat people. They sucked in mountains of tiny shrimp, trapping them behind the hairy plates which they had instead of teeth.

The birds were shearwaters, smallest and toughest of seabirds, and unlike gulls and guillemots they uttered no cries; but as she approached she heard a strange pattering, like rain on a shelter. It was the sound of thousands of shearwater feet running over the waves to take off.

The patter rose to a rush of wings as one edge of the 'island' peeled off the water into the air. The black flock shivered and broke apart as they dived, each bird plucking prey from the Sea, raising a tiny dart of spray – while around them the whales spouted and arched, taking their vast share of the life-giving shrimp which the Sea Mother had sent up from the deep.

There was something dream-like about the mountainous whales and the minute silver darts spiking the waves, the loud slow blows of the greatest of hunters, and the pattering torrent of tiny voiceless birds.

'Renn, it's too dangerous! *Come back!'*

'I have to make them fly! That's what the riddle means!'

She no longer felt the ache in her shoulders. Her skinboat was speeding over the waves.

The shearwaters saw her coming and their raindrop patter rose to a murmur, then a thunder as she swept into the dark cloud of whirling wings. Now the whole island was rising into the sky, she felt as if it was carrying her with it and she too was flying.

Suddenly a gleaming black mountain surged out of the Sea in front of her boat. For an instant she saw the gaping cavern of the whale's mouth, the furrowed trenches of its belly stretched to engulf a lake of prey. She saw the big smooth mound of wet muscle that was its blowhole. Rheu! A column of spray shot skywards, soaking her.

No time to say sorry for disturbing its hunt. The whale's dark eye met hers, and it was wise with the wisdom of the deep: *To me you are a speck of foam on the Sea and I bear you no ill will, but that won't save you…*

As its great back arched to dive, waterfalls poured from its upturned tail. The tip of one giant fluke caught the prow of Renn's skinboat and flicked her high, the boat flying one way, she another.

The last thing she heard before she hit the Sea was the patter of shearwater feet settling back onto the waves, and Naiginn yelling her name.

$|✗T€€N

Renn is cold beyond imagining. Torak's lips are blue as he mouths her name. They are separated by a wall of ice. She hammers with her fists but it's harder than flint, she can't break through. In her head her mother is laughing. *You'll never reach him now...*

Renn woke with a shudder.

She was lying under musty reindeer pelts in freezing gloom. Beside her a rawhide vat. Its urine stink reminded her of the women's part of the Narwal shelter at the clan meet.

Her parka and leggings were gone, she wore a calf-length robe of motheaten seal hide. She still had her spare knife tied to her shin, the duckbone whistle at her neck and Torak's headband round her wrist. Nothing else.

Naiginn's face appeared above her, taut with concern. 'How d'you feel?'

'Like I fell off a cliff,' she mumbled.

'Lucky you didn't break your neck.'

'Is this Waigo?'

He nodded.

'I'm *cold*.'

'I can't bring you inside, it's against the rules.'

Moaning, she turned to the wall, and came face to face with a leg-bone as thick as a log.

She touched it with her finger. A jolt and a surge of heat coursed through her. The air grew bright and fragrant. She knew at once that she was having a vision. She was walking through whispering sedge among grazing herds of the strangest creatures she'd ever seen. Deer taller than elk, horses no bigger than dogs. She was not afraid, for she sensed that she was in the Deep Past, seeing things which once had been.

From across the plain came weird booming shrieks. Huge shaggy brown creatures were ambling towards her. Mammut. Their twisted tusks swept the sedge, and with long supple trunks they gently touched each other's faces. Renn heard their deep slow rumblings like distant thunder. She sensed togetherness and peace.

The vision changed. Clouds darkened the plain and men with poisoned spears chased the mammut over a cliff. Crows pecked carcasses until nothing remained but bleached bones.

'You saw all that?' said Naiginn. The awe and envy in his voice told her she'd described her vision aloud.

'I'm *cold*,' she moaned.

He left, but soon returned and carried her into the blubbery fumes of the men's chamber, where he laid her in a nest of musk-ox wool by a crackling fire.

'How did you manage that?' she murmured.

'I told them you'd seen mammut. They don't believe a woman could have such a vision, so they've decided you have the souls of a man.'

When she woke again she was warm, and aching in every limb. From the smoke-hole hung a carved narwal the size of a hand, smeared with blood-offerings. But this shelter was different from the one at the clan meet. It was built of the massed bones of mammut. Giant ribs supported the smoke-blackened walrus hide. Teeth ringed the fire, each as big as a man's foot. Maybe this far north, only the remains of the sacred beasts could protect the clan from demons.

Like the men he was talking to, Naiginn was bare-chested and seated on part of a mammut backbone. An old woman shuffled towards them. She too was bare-chested, her shrunken breasts swinging like empty pouches as she dragged a mammut shoulderblade piled with slimy dark-red meat. She withdrew and the men ate noisily. Renn was hungry, but no one brought her food.

On the wall behind her, two mammut tusks made a twisted arch, and from it glared a Mage's mask. Painfully she raised herself on her elbow. A mane of red seaweed trailed to the ground, and the painted wooden face was a cormorant's: sharp beak, green slate eyes. At the back of the mask, two strings hung down. By pulling them, the Mage would open the beak to reveal a second face within. The red mane told Renn that this face would be the sun.

Only a Mage of great skill can use a mask with two faces. Renn guessed that when Marupai wore it he became cormorant, and flew to the sun to speak with the spirits. Maybe Naiginn was right, maybe his father could help her.

The old woman was back, clutching a rawhide bowl. Naiginn took it and curtly dismissed the woman. 'Eat,' he told Renn.

A rancid green sludge. 'What is it?' she mumbled with her mouth full.

'Ptarmigan droppings.'

She spat it out. 'You eat *droppings*?'

'Not me, I had *kivyak*, but I'm not a girl. Drink this. It's wormwood, it'll ward off fever.'

After forcing down the bitter brew, she lay back and shut her eyes. 'How did I get here?'

He told her about fishing her out of the Sea. 'You were so pale I thought you were dead.'

'What happened to my boat?'

'Smashed.'

'My gear? Did you salvage anything?'

'What you had on you: medicine pouch, tinder pouch, axe, knife. That whistle which makes no sound.'

'My bow?'

'No.'

She was silent. She hadn't loved it as much as the old one, but it had served her well and it didn't deserve to end its life that way.

'Your disguise washed off,' said Naiginn. 'The elders had never seen anyone like you, they thought you were a demon till I told them you'd seen mammut.'

'Where are my clothes?'

'Your boots are drying, the rest were burnt. They stank.'

'And this robe doesn't?'

He grinned. 'What you did… You really are mad.'

'I solved part of the riddle.'

'Did you get any answers?'

'I don't think it's the kind of riddle that gives them. It sets you tasks which you have to do.'

A man spoke brusquely to Naiginn in Narwal. His bristling moustaches reminded Renn of a walrus.

'Is that your father?' she asked when the man had gone.

'No, he's one of the elders.' He looked worried. 'Marupai isn't here.'

Renn struggled to sit up. 'Where is he?'

'On the Mage's Rock, out to Sea.'

'Then let's go and find him.'

'It isn't that simple, he's gone to work a charm.'

'When's he coming back?' she said uneasily.

'Not till First Dark, when the sun sinks below the Sea.'

'But that's the end of summer! We have to find him now!'

'We can't. Women aren't allowed on the Rock.'

'But they think I've got the souls of a man.'

'In the body of a girl.'

'Tell them I'm a Mage.'

'Women can't be Mages.'

'Yes, they can!'

'Renn, I know my people. Let me think!'

He was silent. Then he snapped his fingers. 'I've got an idea.'

'D'you think you can do it?' Naiginn said under his breath.

Renn glanced at the Narwal elders standing on the blustery hilltop, arms crossed on their chests. 'You never know with ravens. If they do come, will it work?'

'My people respect ravens, they help us find carcasses flung up by the Sea Mother.'

'You stay here, I'll move off a bit. Rip and Rek won't come if I'm with strangers. That includes you.'

The settlement of Waigo occupied a green hill with a commanding view of the Sea. Above a shingle beach a line of skinboats hung from whale-jaw arches, and above these the Narwals' shelters clung like limpets. The hilltop was flat, as if its head had been lopped off. A pile of bleached walrus skulls served both as a lookout post to watch for whale spouts and a beacon to guide the boats home.

Even with Naiginn half-carrying her, Renn had struggled to reach the top. Her head was swimming, her legs limp as seaweed. As she left the men the wind did its best to fling her off the hill. Her calf-length robe shortened her stride and she repressed the urge to get on all fours and crawl.

She made it to a rock on which ravens had smashed guillemot eggs. The blue-green fragments glistened with fresh yolk. Good, the ravens must be near. Provided, of course, that they were Rip and Rek – and provided they heeded her call.

She blew the duckbone whistle.

Clouds scudded across the sky. The elders watched grimly.

She whistled again. *Please, little grandfathers, hear my call! This is no time for tricks!*

Over her shoulder she saw them riding the wind with reckless abandon: Cuckoo! Cuckoo! Sweeping past the elders, they alighted at her feet, snapping their glossy black wings. She bowed a greeting. With throaty croaks, Rip and Rek bowed back. The elders remained inscrutable, but Renn sensed they were impressed.

As abruptly as the ravens had arrived they hopped onto the wind and flew off, loudly cawing cuckoo.

Naiginn was grinning. 'It worked! We can go, as long as you stay in my boat and don't set foot on the Mage's Rock. Hurry, before they change their minds!'

SEVENTEEN

Torak ate a handful of bitter chickweed and a shrivelled mushroom. A surge of nausea. He vomited. Wolf lapped up the sick.

Torak couldn't see the snow owl but he felt it watching. '*Please* give me back my hunting luck!' he begged. 'What must I do to make things right?'

He'd offered earthblood and a lock of his hair, but it hadn't worked. His shots went astray, his snares and fishing lines caught nothing. He'd been reduced to raiding the little mounds on the fells where voles kept their winter food-hoards; but a clutch of tiny haregrass roots wouldn't keep him alive. Soon he'd be too weak to hunt.

He was exhausted from the strain of watching for ice bears, and he couldn't always rely on Wolf to warn him, as stinking springs often masked the scent. Torak hadn't seen the big female again, but he started at every piece of drift ice and every curl of foam. Always when he went ashore he found a menacing line of tracks. Always he felt the unseen presence of the great white owl.

He'd hardly set off again when mist swallowed the coast. Whatever Renn had done to throw Wolf off her trail was still working, but luckily Torak spotted another of Naiginn's markers wedged in a rock rising from the Sea. It was a stick of driftwood pointing the way. He knew it was Naiginn's because of the slanted lines notched in it, like a narwal's tusk. When Torak had seen the first one he'd suspected a trick. Then he'd found traces of their camp and realized it wasn't. *I'll help you in any way I can*, Naiginn had said. Apparently he was keeping his word. This made Torak feel worse. He needed to hate Naiginn, to keep from thinking about Renn.

The mist thinned and the coast reappeared. Torak heard splashing.

It was a sea-eagle and it was drowning, thrashing the waves with waterlogged wings. It was some distance out to Sea and Torak felt so weak that he decided against rescuing it. But it's bad luck to leave a creature dying in a strange way, so he changed his mind.

The eagle was young and had got tangled in a mess of kelp. It *hated* being rescued. Shrieking with outrage, it pecked and lashed out with its talons. Torak grabbed the scrap of reindeer hide he'd been sitting on, flung it over the struggling bird and hauled it aboard. When he'd cut it free it hopped into the bow and stared at him resentfully.

Eagles are proud, but not very bright. This one didn't have the sense to wait for its wings to dry. It tried to fly away and fell off the boat.

With a sigh Torak fished it out.

The eagle hissed at him and jumped overboard.

Again Torak pulled it out. 'Do that once more and you're on your own.'

The eagle was so exhausted it sat hunched in the prow, quietly spitting.

Wolf pushed past Torak and sniffed. The eagle gave an ear-splitting shriek. Wolf decided against risking an eye for a mouthful of feathers and withdrew behind Torak, who was heading for the coast to put the ungrateful bird ashore.

No sooner had he reached the shallows than the sea-eagle jumped onto the shingle, shook its vast wings and wobbled off on the wind.

'And don't come back!' muttered Torak.

Dizzy with hunger, he started for the fells. On a bank above a creek he found a snow owl's lookout: a tussocky patch of red grass enriched by droppings and littered with pellets crammed with fur and bones.

Torak had an idea. With earthblood from his medicine horn he daubed his Forest sign on a pebble. Then he cut off a lock of hair, wound it round the pebble and laid it in the grass. He couldn't see the snow owl, but he knew it was watching.

'Owl,' he called. 'You saw me rescue that sea-eagle! I saved one of your hunters! Forgive what I did and give me back my hunting luck!'

Wolf flicked an ear and looked at Torak. Torak glanced to his right. Wolf slunk that way and disappeared over the ridge. Torak belly-crawled after him.

Before him the mossy fell was speckled with goosedown and fat worm-like droppings – but the flock was a distant white blur at the feet of the mountains. No matter, he would wait for Wolf to drive them closer.

The signs were good. The wind was in his face, so the geese wouldn't smell him; and the moss was pitted with holes where they'd plucked it out by the roots. This meant they'd been grazing heavily, and with luck they'd be too full to fly high.

Wolf had melted into the fells as only a wolf can. Torak pictured him slinking behind the flock so stealthily that no watchful gander could spot him.

Swiftly Torak laid his bow and arrows within reach, untied Orvo's slingstones from his waist and dabbed earthblood on the bone weights.

A faraway honking. The white cloud was rising: Wolf had put them to flight. Torak's heart was pounding. *Don't whirl them above your head*, Dark had taught him. *Cast from your heel, twisting your body and putting your arm into it...*

Wolf had done well, the flock was speeding towards Torak, its shadow racing over the fell. The honking and whirring of wings grew to a rush, and still he kept low: if they saw him all was lost. Now the wind they were making was blowing back his hair. The leader flew overhead. Springing to his feet, Torak whirled the slingstones and threw. The thongs whipped round a goose, the weights clacked, the bird thudded to earth. Grabbing his bow, Torak loosed an arrow, downed another, then another. The flock was so huge he could have shot blindfold, but they flew fast, and as he flung round to shoot again, he hit one last bird before they vanished into the clouds.

Wolf bounded up, lashing his tail. *Good hunt!*

Torak sensed something sweeping overhead. 'Thank you for bringing back my luck!' he called to the snow owl.

Wolf took two geese and Torak kept two for himself. Resisting the urge to rip them open and devour their livers at once, he cut off their heads and took one as an offering to the owl's lookout, leaving the other on a bed of dwarf willow for the Forest. *Then* he cut out the livers.

That first bite: rich, bloody and sweet... He skinned and roasted a bird to eat now, then smoked the other for later, with the hearts and tongues. While Wolf happily demolished his geese, Torak ate and ate, crunching crisp skin and juicy roast flesh, licking fat off his fingers, cramming his mouth till he couldn't manage another bite.

To fulfil the Pact he wrapped the feathers and bones in a goose skin and left it at the snow owl's lookout. Soon afterwards the great bird swooped and carried it off.

Snuggled under the skinboat, Torak lay listening to the crack of embers and Wolf burping contentedly in his sleep. He felt more hopeful than he had in days. Renn had tried to slow him down but it hadn't worked for long.

She would have enjoyed the goose hunt. He pictured her dark eyes fixed on the prey; her straight, strong back as she took aim. Drifting asleep, he imagined they were together in the Forest. He even heard the murmurs of trees.

The day after the goose hunt, he reached Waigo.

His safe-passage stick got him a bowl of rancid walrus in a Narwal shelter, but his questions met with blank stares, and there was no Orvo to translate. 'Marupai? Naiginn? Renn? Rheu?' Nothing. He drew a Sea-eagle tattoo on his hand, but if Renn had been here in disguise, they weren't telling.

Nothing to gain by staying, so he paddled away and put in at the next bay. Another day gone and what had he achieved?

It was so windy he could hardly stand as he carried the skinboat onto the fell. He found scant shelter in the lee of a rocky outcrop with a stream rushing past. He was too angry and frustrated to care.

Wolf was also in a bad mood, scratching furiously. When Torak tried to rub him with bloodstone, Wolf warned him off with a tetchy growl.

The pack-sister was at the Great Den of the Taillesses, he told Torak.

Torak asked where she'd gone, and Wolf's gaze told him what he already knew: north across the Great Wet.

Yes, but *where?*

The sun was low, the charcoal sky shot with angry crimson. Now what? wondered Torak. He couldn't simply head north across the open Sea, he might paddle off the Edge of the World.

Wolf was still scratching.

It occurred to Torak that he always scratched the same place: on his left flank, behind his foreleg.

Suddenly Torak had an appalling idea. Gently he touched Wolf's flank. This time his pack-brother let him. Torak parted the thick fur. It was as he'd thought: Wolf's flank bore the scars of tokoroth claws from his battle three summers before.

Torak felt as if he was falling from a great height. Wolf's scars. Renn's scar on her hand. The scar on his own forearm. All three had one thing in common.

At last Torak knew what Naiginn truly was.

EIGHTEEN

The dark-grey sky was slashed with crimson as Naiginn's skinboat flew over the waves. Waigo had dwindled to a speck. The Mage's Rock was lurching closer. It made Renn giddy, but when she shut her eyes she felt worse.

'Are you sick?' said Naiginn without turning round.

She leant over the side and retched.

'Must be those ptarmigan droppings,' he said.

'I spat them out.'

'Sea-sickness.'

'I'm never sea-sick.' Her head was spinning, his voice coming from far away.

In the distance she saw Rip and Rek teasing a sea-eagle. Their twisting swoops made her dizzier.

When she opened her eyes, Rek was perched on the

side of the boat, peering up at her. Cuckoo, croaked the raven. Cuckoo.

'Why do they keep doing that?' snapped Naiginn.

The raven's fathomless black gaze met Renn's with piercing intent. *Cuckoo*... What was Rek trying to say?

The skinboat swerved and the raven shot skywards, uttering stony warnings: chuk-chuk-chuk!

It took Renn a moment to realize that Naiginn had swept past the Mage's Rock. 'What are you doing?' she cried.

'It's just a rock. Nothing there.'

'But— You said Marupai's doing a rite!'

He laughed. 'I made that up.'

Clutching the sides of the boat, Renn watched the Rock sink beneath the waves. 'Then where is he?'

'Who cares?'

'Where are we going?'

He didn't reply.

Her vision was blurred, her lips numb. With a plunging sensation she remembered the bitter brew he'd given her at Waigo. 'You drugged me,' she mumbled.

'Well done,' he sneered.

When Renn came to, she was lying in front of Naiginn in the bow. Her head was pounding, her wrists tied behind her back.

Naiginn bared his white teeth in a grin. 'I used Torak's

headband. I thought that was fitting, since he's what drew you north.'

Renn tried to sit up and bashed her cheek against the boat. Naiginn watched dispassionately, as if observing the scrabblings of an ant.

'Why are you doing this?' she said.

Laying his paddle across his knees, he flung back his hood and took off his eyeshield. 'Tell me,' he said calmly. 'What do you call a tokoroth when it grows up?'

She swallowed. 'That's never happened.'

'But what if it did? And what if, instead of a tokoroth – instead of some feeble little demon trapped in the worthless flesh of a child – *what if* you found yourself face to face with an all-powerful ice demon in the body of a grown man? What would you call that, *sister?*'

Renn did not reply.

He bent closer and his light-blue eyes were empty and cold beyond imagining, not a spark of human warmth. 'Me.'

Rip and Rek had been trying to tell her for days. *Cuckoo.* The stranger who pretends to be what he is not.

She lay trussed like a goose, watching Naiginn scything the Sea with swift, sure strokes. His eyes were fixed on the skyline. He only appeared human. His face and form were those of a young man, but inside he was demon.

135

No clan-soul, no sense of right or wrong. No feelings whatsoever – except a hatred of all living things and a raging hunger to destroy.

'That's why you don't like earthblood,' she said. 'That's why you hate the smell of bloodstone. You fear it because it smells of the Otherworld, where demons are trapped.'

'I don't fear anything,' he snarled.

'It's why you hate the sun. Because it's stronger than ice.'

'Nothing's stronger than ice! Ice chases the sun into a cave and keeps it there all winter.'

'Then the sun returns and melts the ice.'

'Where I was born the ice never melts.'

'Where's that?'

In his inhumanly perfect features, Renn saw traces of their mother, and although he was silent, she sensed his desire to talk: to boast how he had deceived her. This more than anything convinced her that he truly was Seshru's son. He had the same soaring vanity, the same unshakeable belief that he was stronger and cleverer than everyone else.

She said, 'You told me once that your father met the Viper Mage on the fells. Was that a lie too?'

'Why would I lie about that? She told him she came from the sun, and the lovesick fool believed her. She'd fled north after the Soul-Eaters were scattered, she needed a refuge where she was unknown. Marupai was perfect. She made him do whatever she wanted. Soon he blurted out his precious secret: that he alone of his clan had found

136

the Island at the Edge of the World.' His chin jutted. 'She made him take her there. It's where I was born.'

Renn could tell that in his overweening vanity, he revered the story of his creation. 'She tricked Marupai into believing that as I was a "child of the sun", my spirit would scorch mortals to death unless she hid it with a spell. So while he stayed in camp, she took me to the ice mountain that rules the Island. She snared a great and powerful demon. She trapped it in my infant flesh.'

It began to make sense. Seshru had longed to create a tokoroth, her own demonic creature to obey her will. She'd tried once and failed. What no one suspected was that she'd tried again – and succeeded. She'd captured an ice demon and trapped it in her child.

'But if all this happened when you were a baby,' said Renn, 'how do you know about it?'

'Are you so stupid you've forgotten what I told you? After seven winters she came back! She told me what I am. She promised that when I was a man she would return and set me free to fulfil my destiny: to roam the world, feeding for ever on the souls of the living.' Hungrily he gazed at the skyline, envisioning limitless carnage.

'But she never did come back,' Renn said quietly.

'She *cheated* me!' he shouted. 'I was *glad* when I heard she was dead! Dead like a dog in the dirt, with an arrow in her breast!' His eyes were bloodshot, his face contorted with rage. Renn wondered how she had ever thought him beautiful.

'So why do you need me?'

He shot her a look of freezing hatred. 'What she told Marupai about masking my nature was half-true. When she trapped my demon souls in that filthy, bawling infant, she made a second spell to hide what I really am.'

Renn nodded. 'A masking spell. That's why I never sensed what's wrong with you.'

'There's nothing *wrong* with me, I'm more perfect than you'll ever grasp!'

'That's why Torak didn't sense it either,' Renn said to herself. 'Or Wolf. That's why it made our scars itch: because we got them from tokoroths and the demon bear. But what about Marupai? Surely your own father—'

'He's not my father! That was Seshru's lie, to make him care for me after she left. She made him swear to guard "his son" with his life – and he obeyed. He'll go on pining for his "lost love" till his dying day.'

'But now she's dead, so your demon souls are trapped.'

His face twisted. 'Sixteen winters,' he said bitterly. 'Sixteen winters with "my father" and the other stinking mortals. Sixteen winters surrounded by the living, yet unable to feed. Making do with the shreds of souls that cling to eyes, tongues, heads: the taste and smell but never the souls themselves... Can you *imagine* what that's like? Always famished, never satisfied?'

Renn's mind was racing. She was starting to see why he needed her.

'You're wondering how you fit in,' he said.

'You're right, I am.'

'Of course I'm right, I can read your every thought.'

No, you can't, Renn told him silently. This made her feel stronger. Naiginn was clever, but so was she. Struggling upright, she said, 'So how do I fit in?'

He tightened his grip on the paddle. 'The masking spell that binds my demon souls can only be broken in the place where it was made. And only by a Mage who is bone kin to our mother.'

'Ah. And you can't do Magecraft.'

He hated being reminded. 'When I heard I had a sister who was a Mage, I knew it was meant to be. All I had to do was find a way to bring her north.'

'So that dream Marupai had about your people starving, and the raven with the broken wing—'

He laughed. 'I had to tell you something when I "just happened" to find you floundering in that riptide!'

"And before? How did you "make" me leave the Forest?'

'Easier than I could have dreamt! At first I thought Torak was an obstacle to be eliminated. Then I saw how to use him. Oh, it was beautiful! All I had to do was make you believe you were going to hurt him!'

The pieces were fitting together like pack ice. 'You set that spring-trap. You put the viper in the tree, you planted the signs that sent me north. You scratched Torak's marks on the bark.'

He was shaking with laughter. 'You were so *ready* to believe it! Whining about your mother and your Soul-Eater marrow! I wonder if your dull little human mind can grasp the brilliance of what I did? Can you *see* how I've used your disgusting human weakness – your *love* for your mate – to make you do what I want?'

'But you can't make me do Magecraft.'

'Oh, yes, I can.' Seizing her by the hair, he dragged her face close to his. 'We're going to the Island where I was made. You're going to break the spell and set me free.'

NINETEEN

To catch your prey, you have to think like it. You have to *become* your prey.

Naiginn was a demon. Torak knew that now. And the demon had Renn. With an effort of will, Torak stifled panic. Panic wouldn't help her. Naiginn was his prey: Torak had to find him. This meant he had to think like him, he had to become as a demon and put aside right and wrong.

In all the times he'd ever spirit walked, Torak had never become demon, but he had become snake. And like a demon, a snake knows no right or wrong. It knows no emotion except the urge to kill. To find Naiginn, Torak drew on the ruthlessness the viper had left in his souls. He resolved to break his word to the north wind – and fly.

The wind knew what he meant to do. It screamed in his ears as he overturned the skinboat for a shelter, it clawed his eyes and tore at his hair. 'You can't stop me!' he cried. 'I have to find out where he's taken her!'

It wasn't much of a shelter, wedged in the rocks below the outcrop. Wolf threw him a doubtful glance: *Couldn't you find somewhere better?*

Torak climbed to the topmost rock. It was spattered with droppings and around it he found eagle pellets crammed with bones, feathers and fur. Good. If these pellets had been left by a young eagle like the one he'd rescued, it should be easy to control; if by a full-grown bird, he would find some way to bend it to his will.

To lure the bird to the rocks he tucked scraps of smoked goose heart in cracks, then went and hid under the skinboat.

As he waited for the eagle to take the bait, he enticed Wolf into the shelter with more goose heart. He didn't know enough wolf talk to explain about spirit walking. He couldn't tell Wolf that while his name-soul and clan-soul were flying in the eagle's body, his own body would remain here, unconscious and vulnerable. Instead he simply asked Wolf to watch over him while he slept.

Wolf lay on his belly with his muzzle close to Torak's. Sensing Torak's unease, he snuffle-licked his chin. *I am with you. I never leave.* Torak breathed his pack-brother's meaty breath and stroked his furry flank. He felt the comforting beat of Wolf's tail against his leg. *I know.*

It was two summers since he'd spirit walked, but before leaving the Forest he'd made Dark give him a piece of the black root that loosens souls. Its carrion stink evoked evil memories. Spirit walking is painful and hard. You never know what the other creature's spirit will be like till it's too late and you're in its marrow.

Huddled in the gloom, Torak held the root to his lips and listened to the stream tumbling past the outcrop, the wind battering the skinboat.

He thought of Naiginn's ice-blue eyes and empty smile. He hadn't wanted to touch Torak's medicine horn. All demons fear earthblood; and the horn was made from an antler tine of the World Spirit himself.

But why had Wolf never sensed that Naiginn was a demon? Why hadn't Renn?

And why had Naiginn saved him from being dragged overboard when they were fishing? Why leave those waymarkers for him to find? Did Naiginn *want* him to follow, for some mysterious purpose of his own? Or was he taunting Torak? *You can't catch me, but let's see you try!*

'Oh, I'll try,' Torak said between his teeth. 'I'll keep trying till I find you and if you hurt her I'll rip out your spine.'

Sea-eagles fly quietly. Torak didn't know it had taken the bait until Wolf pricked his ears.

The root was so bitter he could hardly force it down. Darts stabbed his temples. Darkness gnawed his marrow, wrenching his souls loose. He shouted in pain...

...and out of his beak came a screech.

The eagle was *furious*, things kept going wrong, it was so *humiliating*. First he'd fallen in the Sea and been rescued. Now this wobbly landing onto his perch, for a beakful so dry he nearly choked. This shouldn't happen to an eagle, eagles deserve *respect*.

Deep in the bird's marrow, Torak tried to turn its head towards the Sea, but though it was stupid, its spirit was strong.

Like all hunters it was inquisitive, and it had spotted an odd-looking boulder below its perch. Lifting its tail it spattered the skinboat with droppings. Then, jerking its head to sharpen its sight, it spread its wings and hopped onto the wind.

For the second time in his life Torak was flying. As a raven he'd been wild with the joy of flight, but now with an eagle's pride he let the wind carry him higher in an exhilarating spiral. He was the strongest bird in the sky and he flew *fast*, piercing the clouds, challenging the sun itself.

But he was hungry, so he tilted a wingtip and flew level to scan his domain. All lay beneath him and he saw *all* with the keenest sight of any living creature. Every detail was achingly sharp, colours more throbbingly alive than Torak had ever imagined. Through the eagle's eyes he saw the russet flecks of dust on a lemming's paws as it darted for its burrow. He saw the oily green sheen on a cluster of hare droppings, the strident yellow prickles on a caterpillar curled in the moss. He saw a purple water-snail hiding in the stream near the outcrop, and a shard of blue sunlight trapped in an icicle on a distant mountain.

But he couldn't see Naiginn or Renn because the eagle wasn't scanning the Sea, it only had eyes for the land.

Again Torak tried to turn its head seawards – but at that moment the eagle spotted a hare hopping past the skinboat.

The eagle soared higher, Torak saw a jolting blur of clouds – then he was folding his wings in a dive and hurtling towards his prey. Earth rushed towards him at terrifying speed. He swung his talons to snatch the hare.

At the same instant Wolf burst from under the boat and the hare fled. The eagle missed, pulling awkwardly out of its dive and shrieking with rage. How *dare* that wolf go after its prey!

For a third time Torak yanked the eagle's head seawards – and at last he succeeded. He saw every fleck of foam on the waves, every tiny shrimp rising from the deep – and far out on the glittering Sea, he saw Naiginn's skinboat. He saw his streaming hair and the flex of his forearms as he paddled past a fang of black rock. He saw Renn slumped before Naiginn in the bow. Her hair blazed preternaturally red and her eyes were shut, she was terrifyingly pale: not even with the sight of an eagle could Torak tell if she was alive.

With a screech of rage the eagle wrenched its will from Torak's and shot after the hare. Torak saw moss flying from its paws as it zigzagged up a creek. It hadn't seen the eagle, it was fleeing from Wolf, and Wolf's gaze was alight with blood-hunger: he'd forgotten all about guarding his pack-brother.

The hare still hadn't sensed the threat in the sky, but the eagle was too stupid to keep it that way. It swooped from the wrong direction. The hare felt the chill of its shadow and dodged. The eagle missed, swooped again, punching into the hare with both feet, snapping its neck and killing it instantly. Clutching its prey in its talons, the eagle rose triumphantly skywards—

—or it would have done if something hadn't yanked it rudely back to earth.

The eagle gave a furious squawk: what was wrong? Torak was startled to see Wolf gripping the hare's hindquarters in his jaws. *Let go!* Torak shouted from the eagle's marrow.

But the look in his pack-brother's eyes told him that Wolf had no intention of letting go.

Wolf wasn't letting some stupid bird steal his prey. Grimly he tightened his jaws on the hare's hindquarters while the eagle screeched and flapped and clung to its head.

Through a mouthful of hare Wolf gave a muffled snarl as he dragged both eagle and prey over the rocks. The eagle tried to peck, but Wolf was shaking hare and bird from side to side, it couldn't reach. Thrashing its wings, the bird surged into the Up – and suddenly there was no more ground under Wolf's paws, he was kicking at nothing, the eagle was lifting him too.

Still growling, Wolf clawed its feet with his forepaws. The bird bent to peck, and for the flick of a tail they were muzzle to beak and eye to eye. Deep in the eagle's furious stare, Wolf saw a spark that was *not eagle* – and suddenly he knew that this not-eagle was Tall Tailless. *What was Tall Tailless doing inside a bird?*

Wolf was so astonished he let go of the hare and crashed to earth. The eagle soared into the clouds with its prey.

Wolf got to his feet and shook himself. His blood-hunger was gone. His hindpaw hurt. The chase had taken him many lopes over the treeless lands – and by the smell of it, a long way from Tall Tailless.

Tall Tailless.

Suddenly Wolf remembered that he was supposed to guard his pack-brother.

Worry gnawed his belly as he limped up a ridge to see where he was. Far across the fells he spotted the rocks where Tall Tailless had made his den. The angry wind had carried away the floating hide, and Wolf saw Tall Tailless curled on his side, fast asleep.

Then Wolf saw something that made his pelt prickle with dread.

Prowling towards his slumbering pack-brother was a great white bear.

TWENTY

Torak fell screaming from the clouds and hit the ground with a thud.

As always after spirit walking it took him a while to come to, and though his body was unhurt, his souls were badly bruised from the fall.

He became aware of a murmurous rustling. He knew that sound. It was the voices of trees. But surely the eagle hadn't carried his spirit all the way back to the Forest?

The sounds were unmistakeable: whispering willows, chattering birch... He'd missed them terribly, but now he was horrified. Instead of finding out where Naiginn had taken Renn, he'd goaded the wind into blowing his souls south.

And yet – he was in his body again. He smelt earth, he was lying with his face in cold wet leaves.

Opening his eyes, he found himself looking *down* at the Forest from a great height. Between fluffy white clouds he saw tiny green trees. How could this be? Was he still flying?

His gaze shifted to a pallid mountain of bones – and he understood. The mountain was an eagle pellet, the clouds were tiny catkins. He hadn't been blown anywhere, he was still in the Far North, lying at the foot of the outcrop – *and the Forest was here too.*

It had always been here, but he'd never thought of it as Forest, he'd simply walked unheeding over these springy mats of stunted willow and birch that covered the fells as densely as the Forest where he was born.

His gaze roamed over miniature hills and valleys covered in trees. Their trunks were no thicker than his finger and they clung flat to the earth amid lichen and moss. Their leaves were smaller than a baby's fingernails – green, amber and red all on the same bough, with catkins and hairy brown fruit – because here in the Far North the days of sunlight are not long: spring, summer and autumn rushing by in only two moons.

But they were still trees, and this Forest of the North was as ancient and wise as the Forest of the South. Torak's eyes ached with unshed tears. All his life the Forest had helped him. It had given him everything he needed to survive, it had never let him down. And it was with him now, its green souls cleansing his spirit like clear water.

149

The wind was tugging his hair with icy fingers. Where was the skinboat?

As he heaved himself to all fours, the outcrop spun wildly and he retched. His souls hadn't recovered from their fall. He spotted the boat in the distance where the vengeful wind had carried it. He didn't care: he'd just solved the second part of the riddle.

To find what you seek, you must cross the Forest in the treeless land. Where he was kneeling now *was* the 'Forest in the treeless land'. Crossing it would be easy, all he had to do was make his way to the boat.

'Easy,' he said.

But no riddle is easy. That's why it's a riddle. As Torak summoned the strength to stand, an ice bear emerged soundlessly from behind the rocks.

⋀⋁⋀

A hunting bear doesn't snarl or champ its jaws, it comes on in lethal silence. That's what the ice bear did now.

It was the huge female with the scarred nose who'd peered at Torak from the clifftop; who'd stared at him as she swam past after fighting the walrus on the beach.

No sign of her cubs, she must have left them in the hills before stalking this troublesome prey which had eluded her twice before.

Halting three paces from Torak, she threw up her long neck and slid out her purple-grey tongue to taste his scent.

He saw the dark teats in her coarse yellow belly fur, he saw her massive turned-in forepaws with their vicious black claws. She couldn't be hungry, her muzzle and neck were stained brown with blubber – but she was a hunter, and hunters never pass up an easy kill.

Still kneeling, Torak grabbed his axe. He knew he wouldn't have time to use it. If she charged she'd be on him in a heartbeat. She would seize his skull in her jaws and snap his neck with a single shake.

Lowering her head, she locked eyes with his. He didn't dare blink. That flat black stare didn't see a boy, it saw a bloody mess of flesh to drag back to her cubs.

He tried to think what to do, but his mind had gone as blank as the sky. Inuktiluk had told him how to avoid encountering an ice bear, not what to do if one got this close. Perhaps he hadn't thought Torak would be stupid enough to let that happen.

What was it Tanugeak had said? *If you survive it'll be by thinking like other creatures.*

Torak knew how hunters thought, he was a hunter too. He knew that ice bears aren't as clever as wolves, but they don't need to be, they're so much stronger. None of this told him what to do.

Slitting her eyes, the ice bear moved her head up and down. Like all hunters she was wary, she went for the weak and the sick. She wouldn't attack healthy prey which fought back, she wouldn't risk breaking a bone or losing an eye. What kind of prey was this?

Ice bears eat seals, Torak thought suddenly. Seals lie low and still on the ice, just as he was doing now. Lurching to his feet, he made himself as tall and un-seal-like as he could. He brandished his axe, never taking his eyes from the bear's.

He opened his mouth to shout – then shut it. If he shouted, would she think he was bluffing? If he kept silent, would she see him as a threat? Each bear is different: some run from a threat, some attack. Which was she? What should he *do*?

The bear was sniffing loudly. With a jolt of terror Torak realized he was dressed from head to toe in seal hide. He could see her thinking: *It doesn't act like a seal but it smells like one...*

His mind darted in panic. Was there *nothing* she feared?

Suddenly he remembered the dead bear he'd found by the creek with the tusk wounds in its flank. He saw the bull walrus fighting off this very female, lashing out with its tusks. He heard the clack of tusks on rock. If he made that noise...

No rocks within reach, but he spotted a reindeer antler overgrown with moss. Ripping it free, he bashed it against his axe-handle.

The ice bear shifted from paw to paw. She knew that sound. This prey didn't *look* like a walrus, or smell like one, but it sounded as if it had tusks.

Again Torak clashed antler on wood, and again.

The bear's growls shook the earth beneath him.

'*I'm a walrus!*' he bellowed, clacking his 'tusks'. '*Go away! I'll fight!*' If this didn't work, he was finished.

The bear peeled back her black lips and hissed. She champed her jaws with a noise like clashing rocks. She took a step back.

All at once she swung round as if she'd been bitten.

Wolf flew at her, snapping her rump. With a snarl she went for him. Wolf dodged, darted in to nip her heels. *Run!* his eyes told Torak.

But Torak wasn't about to abandon his pack-brother. Yelling and swinging his axe, he sprang at the bear. She decided that two against one wasn't worth it and bounded for the hills, showing her big black hind pads.

Wolf's apology knocked Torak flat. *Sorry I left you! Sorry!* Nibble-nuzzling Torak's chin, he covered his face in rasping licks.

Torak tried to get up but his legs wouldn't obey. He was dizzy and sick, his souls still shaken.

The bear might be gone, but the skinboat was unreachably far away. How could he trudge across that windswept waste when he couldn't even stand?

Wolf was gazing at the boat with narrowed eyes. *Uff!* But he didn't say it as if he smelt bear. He was puzzled.

Torak squinted at the skinboat. It had grown legs. It was walking towards him.

TWENTY-ONE

Once when Tall Tailless was injured, Wolf had seen his Breath-that-Walks leave his body. This time Wolf had seen it fly, then crash to earth. Now that the bear was gone, Tall Tailless lay with his muzzle in the moss. His Breath-that-Walks was battered and bruised.

Guilt sank its teeth into Wolf's guts. *This was his fault.* He'd chased that hare instead of protecting his pack-brother. And now the two strange taillesses were coming. Wolf could only see the little female's legs, as she was carrying the floating hide. The old one smelt of droppings and his eyes were as white as a well-chewed bone: he couldn't see.

Wolf growl-barked a warning: *Stay away!*

Clutching a stick, the old one halted a few lopes from where Wolf stood over his pack-brother. The half-grown female put down the floating hide and ran to Tall Tailless. Wolf growled louder. The female crouched respectfully low, avoiding his stare. One of her forepaws was twisted. Wolf smelt that she was anxious and at the bottom of her pack – but that she wanted to help Tall Tailless. He moved aside.

She was clever and quick. In the twitch of a tail she'd made a Den over Tall Tailless and woken a Bright Beast-that-Bites-Hot, then helped the Sightless One inside. Wolf tried to follow, but the Sightless One jabbed him with his stick. Wolf didn't like this tailless but he felt sorry for him, for he sensed that bitterness lay on his spirit like a stone.

In the Den the Sightless One began yowling: he too was trying to help Tall Tailless. At least – Wolf thought he was. He decided to keep watch at the mouth of the Den. At the first sniff of trouble he would attack.

Torak was floating naked in scorching steam. He couldn't breathe. Something was pressing on his nose and mouth.

'It's a sweat bath,' whispered a girl. 'Breathe through the moss, it'll stop your lungs burning.'

As he sucked air, he became aware of thin rippling music that twisted round itself like flame. He caught a stink of dung. Opening his eyes, he saw a tiny spurt of fire on a pebble. It sputtered and sank to a violet glow. The glow blinked out, leaving crimson droplets and smoke that smelt of rotten eggs. Bloodstone.

The flute broke off and a shaggy old man leant over him. Matted hair, beard crawling with lice, stumps of teeth as brown as peat. Blind, clouded eyes. Clutching the wing of a diverbird in his grimy talons, the old man passed it over Torak's forehead, then flung it away. The pain in his bruised souls eased. This old man was a Mage.

'Marupai?' gasped Torak.

The old man barked at him in Narwal.

'You're Marupai the Narwal Mage—'

'Not any more. They threw me out when I went blind.'

'But you are Naiginn's father? Where is he? Where's he gone!'

'Who are you? Why are you after my son?'

Torak hesitated.

'Who *are* you? What name d'you carry?'

'Torak.'

The old man blew his nose in his hand and wiped it in his beard. 'I thought you were a demon, I was going to strangle you. Then I touched you and felt eagle. My guide was eagle. But you're no Mage.'

'I'm a spirit walker.'

He snorted, unimpressed. 'Why are you after my son?'

'He's … helping my mate.'

'That's a lie!' Seizing a waterskin, Marupai drenched him in freezing water, grabbed his staff and crawled out of the shelter.

Someone thrust Torak's clothes into his arms. He recognized the girl with the withered arm from the clan meet. By the time he'd dressed, she'd followed her master outside.

Torak found them by the stream. Marupai was casting gobbets of blubber as offerings. The girl crouched nearby, watching Wolf snap them up.

The old man heard Torak approach. 'Wart says your dog's eating my offerings.'

'My dog?' Torak was startled. Then he remembered that Narwals hated wolves. He threw the girl a questioning glance. Was she protecting Wolf? 'I'm sorry about your offerings,' he said carefully.

Marupai grunted. 'If a dog eats an offering it's good, means it's possessed by an ancestor.' He swayed, and the girl moved to help. 'I can manage!' With his staff he struck her a vicious blow on the back.

Despite the cold he was bare-chested and barefoot. His leggings were filthy sealskin stained yellow at the crotch. He reminded Torak of the Walker, the mad old man who wandered the Forest – but Marupai wasn't mad. He was bitter and deluded, bent on protecting his son. 'Tell me the *truth*,' he snarled. 'Why are you after my boy?'

'He and my mate are half-brother and -sister. They had the same mother—'

'*That's a lie!* My beautiful one came from the *sun*! Out of a blaze of light she came to me – *me*! I was the only mortal man she ever took for her mate!'

'She didn't come from the sun, she came from the Forest—'

Marupai lunged at him with his staff. Wolf grabbed it in his jaws and shook. Torak gave a low grunt-whine and Wolf let go. He went on growling. 'It's the truth,' said Torak.

'The *truth!*' sneered the old man. 'Yes, like that wolf of yours is a dog!' He hawked and spat. 'Doesn't matter why you're after my son, he's gone.'

'What do you mean?'

'He left four moons ago. I sent Wart to the clan meet but he wasn't there. She heard he'd gone north but she missed him among the islands. Fool!' Again he lashed out, though this time the girl dodged. 'My finding charms failed,' he muttered. 'My spirit guide has deserted me. What use is an eagle who can't see?'

Torak was aghast. 'You mean you've no idea where he's gone?'

Marupai wasn't listening. He was clutching his head. 'Wart, lead me to the shelter. Soon I will seek my death.'

'He won't sleep long,' muttered the girl.

'How long?' Torak paced up and down. The red sun was getting low, and Renn was out there with a demon in human form.

What if he never saw her again? He pictured himself finding his way back to the Forest. He would go on hunting with the wolves, but without Renn – without his fierce, brave, secretive, complicated Raven – he would never be more than half-alive.

In the shelter Marupai's snores stuttered to a halt, then resumed. Marupai was what Torak would become if he lost Renn.

The girl called Wart was plucking a pair of snow geese by the fire. Torak asked her if she knew where Naiginn had gone.

'If I knew I'd tell you.'

'What's your real name?'

She paused, as if trying to remember. 'Shamik.'

Plucking birds was Torak's least favourite task because the lice ran up his arms, but he threw himself down and grabbed the other goose.

'That's women's work,' said Shamik.

'Not in the Forest.'

Wolf ran to sniff her calloused feet, and she froze like a ptarmigan hiding among rocks. 'He won't hurt you,' said Torak. To his surprise, Wolf was wagging his tail. He was rarely this at ease with strangers. Torak said, 'I thought Narwals hated wolves.'

Her squirrelly face creased in a frown. 'Once I saw a white wolf on the fell. He looked at me and I saw his golden eyes. He was no demon.'

'How come you speak Southern?'

'I'm Ptarmigan.' Behind the bone disc that hung from her upper lip her mouth was a taut unsmiling line. 'They were going to drown me because of this.' She raised her withered arm. 'Instead they traded me cheap when I was five. That's how Narwals get females.'

Torak had wondered. In the Forest when a boy and girl wanted to mate, they could choose either to keep their own clan or join their mate's. It made sense that as Narwals treated women so badly they had to trade for them.

Deftly Shamik gutted her goose. She was small but tough, like the stunted willows of the fells, and though her arm was withered, it still worked. The shelter she'd built was a cunning assembly of split walrus hides over Torak's skinboat and a boulder. Having dealt with the geese, she left two of their feet as an offering, then tented her motheaten robe over her knees and gnawed the remaining two.

In the shelter, the snores stopped. Shamik paused in mid-chew. 'He's waking up.'

'You saw him *today*?' exploded Marupai, showering Torak with spit. 'Why didn't you say?'

'You wouldn't listen.'

The clouded eyes narrowed. 'How did you meet him?'

'It was after the clan meet. He saved my life when we were fishing—'

'How?'

Torak began to explain, but when he mentioned Naiginn's sink-stone the old man cut in. 'You're telling the truth, I taught him that knot. Where was he when you saw him last?'

Torak told him about spirit walking in the eagle. 'He was heading north past a rock like a fang—'

'*No!*' screamed Marupai. 'My poor boy!'

'You know where he's going?'

He was rocking, clawing his mane. 'When I was young I flew to the world of the spirits. I saw the ice bear with eight paws. I swam into the deeps and fetched walruses caught in the Sea Mother's hair...'

Torak stirred impatiently. Shamik gave him a warning look.

'I flew up and touched the moon,' the old man went on. 'I learnt that it's a great disc of ice eternally spinning, so that at times we only see its edge... But above all things I longed to find the island at the Edge of the World.'

Torak stiffened. The Boat Leader's words came back to him: *Far over the Sea lies the Island no Narwal has ever seen. It is said that fiery cracks gape on the Otherworld. Only the spirits of long-dead mammut keep the demons inside...*

'I found it.' Marupai's voice was flinty with pride. 'I alone of mortal men have seen the spirits of mammut walking into the clouds—'

'Is that where Naiginn's taken Renn?'

'Who is Renn?'

'My mate! Is that where he's gone?'

Marupai's grimy features were twisted with pain and longing. 'She was so beautiful the moon stayed behind all day, and the whales swam onto the shore to look at her...'

'Tell me about the Island!'

'One night I told her I'd found it. She made me take her there.'

Torak's spine prickled.

'A terrible place for mortal man, but not for her.' Marupai shuddered. 'There she bore our son. She took him to a sacred cave where no mortal may go. She made a masking spell to hide his blazing spirit, so that the sun in him wouldn't scorch us mortals to death.'

That sounded like Seshru: skilled at lies and half-truths.

'My poor beautiful son,' groaned Marupai. 'She promised to return when he was a man and set his souls free – but the Softbellies murdered her. Now his spirit is bound for ever. I *told* him there was no hope! The spell could only be broken where it was made, and only by a Mage of his mother's bone kin! And what Mage is bone kin to the sun?'

Torak's mind was racing. Once Naiginn had forced Renn to break the spell, he would have no further use for her. He would kill her. 'Tell me how to find the Island.'

Marupai drew himself up. 'I can't.'

'You must!'

'I can't *tell* you how to find it, no words can! My son is in danger. I'll take you there myself.'

TWENTY-TWO

'I can hear the Island calling to me,' said Naiginn.

Renn couldn't hear anything except the slap of waves and the sweep of his paddle – and that was muffled by fog. Icebergs loomed. The setting sun was turning the fog red. As Naiginn steered between them it darkened to violet, then deep, glacial blue. He flicked out his tongue to taste the gloom. 'The night of First Dark. Soon it'll be winter and the ice will swallow the sun.'

The icebergs were left behind. The skinboat slid between eerie white discs of drift ice like fallen moons.

This is the Edge of the World, thought Renn. Her arms ached from being pinioned behind her back. Torak's headband bit into her wrists. The only plan she'd come up with was to kick Naiginn overboard; but if that capsized the boat, she would drown too.

'There it is!' he cried. 'The Island where I was born!'

All Renn could see through the fog was a bank of cloud on the horizon. Her heart contracted. That wasn't cloud, it was ice: a flat, frozen mountain flung by the World Spirit to crush the land beneath.

Howling in triumph, Naiginn brandished his paddle. As he powered the skinboat closer, Renn heard the din of waterfalls and the boom of ice. Suddenly the mountain was blasting them with freezing breath, tossing the boat like a leaf. Her teeth were chattering, but Naiginn exulted in the cold. 'It's making me stronger!'

Ice cliffs towered over them, waterfalls thundering from the heights. On either side of the mountain, Renn saw smoky black headlands clawing the Sea, and a distant red glare. She recalled something Tanugeak had said: *The earth is rent and slashed, its open wounds blaze with the fires of the Otherworld. Only the spirits of long-dead mammut prevent the demons' escape...*

Fearlessly Naiginn paddled into the chill shadow of the ice mountain. Craning her neck, Renn saw its craggy face scarred with cracks. A vast maw gaped on darkness as deep as a midwinter sky. It was fanged with icicles as tall as trees, and spewed an angry torrent into the Sea.

'I was made in that cave,' Naiginn said proudly. 'That's where you'll break the spell and set me free.'

One of the ice fangs broke off with a crash. Spume shot skywards, a wave reared towards the boat. With a whoop Naiginn steered out of its path.

Renn's courage abandoned her. When she was seven winters old, ice had killed her father. Since then it had twice tried to kill her: once when she'd fought the Soul-Eaters in the Far North and once during a storm in the Forest. If she entered that cave, she would never come out. The mountain would snap shut and her souls would be trapped in endless dark.

As suddenly as they'd entered the icy blast, they were clear. The Sea turned milky green as Naiginn neared an inlet of glinting black stones.

'I will never go inside that cave,' said Renn.

He laughed. 'You don't have a choice.'

'You saw that ice-fall. You might have the souls of a demon, but your body is as mortal as mine: if you try to go in there you'll die too.'

'I know another way in.'

He threw her on the shore and carried the boat up the beach, leaving her where she lay; they both knew she had nowhere to run.

The air was hazed with dirty smoke and the rotten-egg smell of bloodstone. Tortured black rocks made her think of bound and blinded giants struggling to break free. In the distance she heard an echoing bellow. Was that the ice mountain, or some demon of the Otherworld fighting to escape?

She had never felt so alone. Rip and Rek had forsaken her, Torak and Wolf belonged to a lost world. Since sighting this Island she hadn't seen a single seal or fish or bird, not one blade of grass. This was no place for living creatures. It was the haunt of demons and ghosts.

And yet, as she struggled to her knees, she had the oddest thought. *What would Seshru do?*

Naiginn returned. Yanking off her boots, he tossed them in the shallows. He spotted the knife bound to her shin and took that too. Having checked her for more hidden weapons, he reached for the medicine pouch at her belt.

'Careful,' she warned. 'I'll need it to break the spell. I'll need my sewing kit too.'

'If you try to trick me I'll know it and I'll hurt you.'

'I won't.'

He grasped the duckbone whistle at her neck.

'I'll need that too.'

'Why, what does it do?'

'It's for calling the spirits. Leave it alone.' Magecraft was the only power she had over him: she could do it, he could not. 'If you want me to break the spell, I have to gather the things I'm going to need.'

'I'm not untying you.'

'Then you have to do it for me.'

He stood clenching and unclenching his fists. 'What d'you need?'

She had the glimmerings of an idea. That Mage's mask at Waigo with two faces... 'Fronds of kelp. An oyster shell or a clam shell: the roundest and whitest you can find.'

'What for?' he said suspiciously.

'Our mother bound your demon souls behind an invisible

mask. I have to turn myself into a raven and peck it off.'

'Why the shell?'

'Because,' she said with exaggerated patience, 'a shell is like the moon, and the moon is always changing, so it will help me change too. You've lived with a Mage, surely you know that?'

He shot her a look of pure hatred – but he did what she said. He'd lost some of his swagger, and when he'd found the kelp and the shell and stuffed them in his parka, he cast about as if unsure where to go.

'You said you knew another way to the ice cave,' said Renn. 'I don't think you do.'

'Shut up.'

'You've never been here without your father, have you?'

'I told you, Marupai's not my father! My father was a Soul-Eater.'

'Hasn't it occurred to you that our mother might have lied about that too?'

'It's true! He was Seal Clan, the greatest hunter they ever had! That's why I'm the best in the world!'

'What a shame you can't do Magecraft.'

He hit her and she fell, bashing her shoulder on a rock. He hauled her to her feet, tied rope round her neck like a leash, then started up the shore, dragging her like a dog. He did it all without expression, and Renn knew that to him she was merely a carcass. He needed her to break the spell, and if she refused, he would maim her till she obeyed – and he would do it as readily as if he were snapping a branch or gutting a fish. He was a demon: he didn't care how living creatures felt. He wanted to eat their souls.

She reminded herself that although he was stronger, he couldn't do Magecraft and he couldn't know her thoughts. He was adept at lies and trickery – but so was she. They both had that from their mother.

And as Renn stumbled after him over the sharp black stones, she remembered something else about Seshru. The Viper Mage had been vicious, cold-hearted and deceitful. But she had never, ever given up.

TWENTY-THREE

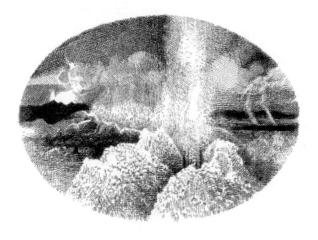

'Keep up!' Naiginn yanked Renn's leash as he changed direction. He was climbing fast, over ridges of black basalt, but now and then he made a sudden turn that rubbed her neck raw. What was he trying to avoid?

Stones cut her feet and her calf-length robe shortened her stride. Wind gusted stinking smoke in her eyes, and an ugly thickening in the air told her demons were near. She could hear them hissing under the earth, but she sensed more flitting free. Not even the spirits of mammut could keep them all in the Otherworld.

And the Otherworld was alarmingly close. Under her feet she felt its unclean heat. This brittle black crust was all that protected her from the blazing horror beneath.

Another tug on the leash. Why did he keep changing direction?

The hissing grew louder as they scaled the next ridge. Again Naiginn turned, but this time Renn resisted. She managed a couple of steps and the ground grew *hot*.

Before her gaped a steaming, bubbling wound in the earth, scabbed with festering yellow. The demon was trapped in the Otherworld, but near the surface, spitting fury and venting venomous smoke. Its breath was a knife in Renn's brain, rasping her throat, obliterating sight. She couldn't stop coughing, couldn't stop gulping scorching smoke.

With a snarl Naiginn slung her over his shoulder and carried her down the slope, then flung her to the ground. 'Do that again and I'll break your arms!'

Lying on her back, she gave a spluttery laugh. 'They frighten you, those holes the demons have clawed. You're scared of them!'

'I'm not frightened of anything! On your feet!'

'Oh, but you are...' She broke off to cough. 'That's where you belong. In the Otherworld with the rest of your kind.'

He raised his fist to strike.

'Careful,' she warned. 'You need me to break the spell!'

'But not necessarily in one piece. Remember that.'

The wounds in the earth were left behind. Naiginn led her through a desolate gully of blasted rock. Renn couldn't see the ice mountain, but its breath chilled her sweat-soaked skin. Soon they would reach the cave – and then what? Her plan seemed doomed to fail.

Naiginn halted. Ahead loomed an immense, half-charred skeleton. A ribcage as big as a shelter, a skull like a boulder, two huge tusks curving out, then in.

'Mammut,' said Renn.

He flinched. He hated even the name.

From far away came the echoing shriek she'd heard from the Sea. She'd heard the same sound in her vision at Waigo. 'The spirits of mammut are strong,' she said quietly. 'They have the power of the Deep Past. No wonder you fear them.'

'I don't fear mammut, they fear me. My poison works fast.' He touched the quiver at his back. But as he edged past the skeleton, he kept close to the wall of the gully, and grimaced when mammut ash drifted over his boots.

'All those mammut bones in the shelters at Waigo,' said Renn. 'Must have been hard for a demon like you.'

'My mother's spell protected me.'

'But not completely,' she guessed.

'Enough!'

They reached a ridge of hard-packed grit that crumbled at every step. Naiginn sank knee-deep, Renn floundered in choking clouds of dust.

She barked her shin on a buried rock. On impulse she screamed and dropped to the ground. 'My leg! I've broken my leg!'

'Get up!' growled Naiginn, tugging the leash.

Still screaming, she ignored him. He stooped to haul her upright. She kicked him in the chest, knocked him backwards down the slope, then sprang to her feet and fled.

'You might as well give up!' Naiginn's voice echoed from ridge to ridge. Renn couldn't tell where he was. She could hardly see for the demon breath billowing around her.

Rocks loomed through the smoke, leaning crazily. She hid behind one: panting, her feet bleeding and burnt. With her hands tied behind her and her leash trailing on the ground, she felt as helpless as a fledgling fallen from its nest.

'I will find you!' called Naiginn with lazy confidence. 'I won't hurt you so much if you give yourself up.'

As far as she could tell she was heading back the way they'd come. Somewhere before her lay the inlet and his boat.

She floundered up another ridge of crumbly black grit. Or was it the same one? Was she running in circles?

With nightmare slowness she stumbled down the other side. The ground at the bottom was hot; demon breath thick with malice, sapping courage. She fought the urge to cough. She heard the seething hiss of the Otherworld, but no taunts from Naiginn. At any moment he might appear, grinning at her from above.

She hadn't gone far when something bit her foot and she was blasted by the foul heat of the Otherworld. She'd nearly fallen into a fissure in the earth as big as a skinboat. She came to another. They were everywhere, deep wounds spitting fierce yellow slime. She didn't remember this place. Where was the gully and the mammut skeleton?

The wind changed. Demon breath engulfed her. She broke into uncontrollable coughing.

Naiginn shouted in glee. 'The demons are helping me! They're telling me where you are!'

Renn ran blindly. The smoke thinned. She glimpsed a fang of black flint, slumped against it, tried in vain to stifle her coughs.

Footsteps crunched closer. 'Not long now!' he taunted.

At the corner of her eye, a shadow slunk behind the rocks. *You're finished*, cackled the demon. *Weaponless, barefoot, trussed like a fowl...*

She repressed a mad impulse to bring this horrible hunt to an end: to step out from her hiding-place and get it over with.

Someone coughed. She jerked round. Nothing there.

'I can hear you!' called Naiginn, terrifyingly close.

But he wasn't the one who'd coughed. It had sounded lighter, like a girl.

There it was again, although whoever it was now sounded further off, and Naiginn's footsteps were hastening after them.

A bird lit onto the rock above her. Rip cocked his head and fixed her with his piercing raven stare – then coughed, perfectly mimicking her. Hitching his wings, he disappeared into the smoke. Moments later, 'Renn's' cough sounded again, far to her right.

She squared her aching shoulders. She was *not* alone. The ravens were with her, using mimicry to lead Naiginn astray.

They'd turned her luck in another way too. Part of the black flint had shattered, littering the ground with shards. Squatting awkwardly, she grabbed one. Its edges were knife-sharp; but try as she might, she couldn't bend her fingers far enough to cut the rawhide at her wrists.

Clutching the shard, she rose to her feet. She couldn't stay here, Naiginn would soon discover the ravens' trick.

A mammut skeleton loomed into sight. It wasn't the same as the one that had unsettled him in the gully. It wasn't as big and the skull was riddled with cracks. Renn saw at once how she could use it. Wedging her flint in a crack, she moved her wrists up and down the fixed blade. She couldn't see what she was doing, felt blood trickling over her hands, but the flint was so sharp it didn't hurt.

The bindings snapped. She cut the hated rope from her neck. She was *free*. She was Renn again, not some bound and beaten thing to be dragged on a leash.

Having tied the rope round her waist, she stuffed the flint in her medicine pouch with Torak's headband. Before her another gritty ridge. She no longer felt the pain in her neck and wrists, or her bloodied and blistered feet. Soon she would find Naiginn's skinboat and escape.

At the top of the ridge she halted. Below her lay a bleak, smoke-filled plain of charcoal rock. Here and there, a distant glimmer of fire. She'd never seen this place. It wasn't the way she'd come.

'It's over, Renn,' shouted Naiginn from the smoke.

Wind blew the icy breath of the mountain in all directions. Clouds hid the sun. She was lost.

And through the demon breath a mountainous shape was lurching towards her.

TWENTY-FOUR

Wolf scrambled ashore while Torak clung to the rocks, fighting to keep hold of the skinboat. The Sea wrenched it from his hands and smashed it beyond repair.

The wind had punished him for daring to fly. It had blown him off course and stranded him – where? Somewhere on the east coast of the Island at the Edge of the World, entombed in dense, freezing fog.

He poured seawater from his boots and checked his gear. He still had his weapons and sleeping-sack, with the pouch of dried ptarmigan tongues Shamik had given him. She'd also given him a waterskin made of walrus gut; on the journey he'd filled it with ice and slipped it under his parka to melt. To steady himself he took a few sips and gave some to Wolf.

The fog was so thick he couldn't see his outstretched hand. He asked Wolf if he smelt demons. Wolf said yes, but not close.

Can you smell the Great Hard Cold?

Not close.

The old tailless and the half-grown female?

No.

The pack-sister?

Wolf's amber gaze grazed his, then slid away. *No.* Torak shut his mind to what that might mean.

They had set off for the Island in two boats: Torak and Wolf in one, Shamik and Marupai in a craft they kept near the shore. Shamik had led the way while Marupai hunched in the prow like a blind old eagle, fingering a tangle of knotted cords that he called his map.

Now and then he'd barked a command: 'East at the headland shaped like a triple-barbed harpoon…' 'Tell me when you spot the next isle, I'll need to smell the coves…' And finally: 'You'll know it's close when you see the ice-blink.' This turned out to be a bank of strangely radiant clouds, which told them that the ice-covered Island lay beneath, glaring up at the sky.

As they'd paddled towards it they'd heard the clamour of waterfalls and the creak and boom of ice. With a growl Wolf had sprung to his feet: *Demons!*

Torak hadn't been able to drag his eyes from the harsh

glitter of the mountain and its dreadful blue cliffs. Was Renn trapped in there? Had Naiginn already forced her to break the spell?

'Stay west of the cliffs!' shouted Marupai, but the wind and the current were dragging Torak *east* – and suddenly he couldn't see the others and the fog's clammy white arms were drawing him in...

Wolf's cold nose on his hand nudged him back to the present. Wolf's hackles were up and his mouth was tense. Torak asked if he smelt ice bears. *No bears, no wolves. Strange prey. Where are we?*

Torak heard waves slapping rocks and the clink of drift ice, but the waterfalls were muted by distance and he caught no sound from the ice mountain. His belly turned over. Had the wind carried them that far away?

The ground rose steeply. All Torak could hear was the creak of his clothes and the click of Wolf's claws.

The fog had darkened to grey. The sun had gone to sleep for the first time: a chilling reminder that winter was not far off.

Wolf had vanished in the murk. Torak groped his way forwards. Maybe his next step would take him over the Edge of the World. Maybe Naiginn had already got what he wanted and flung Renn screaming into the void...

The rocks levelled, the fog cleared a little, and Torak

heard the chatter of water. Wolf was racing about, sniffing the muddy banks of a stream. *Strange prey.*

Torak halted. His hunter's eye told him that something big had trampled the mud – and yet he saw no print of hoof or paw.

He found a clot of hair snagged on a boulder. He pulled out a strand as long as his arm. Higher up on the boulder, a band had been worn smooth. He'd seen such marks in the Deep Forest, where bison used boulders as scratching-posts. But no bison had rubbed these marks. Whatever had made them had stood as tall as a man standing on the shoulders of another.

Wolf was sniffing a shallow indentation in the mud as big as a Mage's drum. Torak stooped to examine it. His spine tingled. Four rounded dents at the front edge were unmistakeably toes. He remembered the painted mammut in the Narwals' shelters; the giant foot jutting from the riverbank.

He spotted more of the huge round footprints. The mammut's stride was so long that Torak could barely leap from one print to the next. Spirits don't leave tracks. The mammut who'd made these prints was alive.

An eerie shriek rang through the fog. Torak and Wolf exchanged startled glances. It sounded like … like an elk, or the Raven Clan's birch-bark horns – but far more powerful.

Warily they headed upstream. Somewhere in this fog was the biggest creature on earth: a creature about whom Torak knew nothing at all.

Wolf caught a scent and loped ahead with eager grunt-whines. Torak ran to keep up – and suddenly he was out of the fog, into dazzling sunlight under a bright blue sky.

Below him stretched an endless, rippling sea of green grass. His astonished gaze took in herds of grazing reindeer and musk-oxen; silver willows fringing gleaming rivers. And far away, the glare of the ice mountain.

With a tightening of his innards he realized what this meant. On this side, the mountain sent rivers to water these lush green plains – but on the other side, the side he'd seen on reaching the Island, it reared above the Sea in those dreadful blue cliffs.

The wind had carried him much further up the coast than he'd feared. It had stranded him on the wrong side of the mountain – and Renn, if she was still alive, was somewhere on the other.

Wolf *thought* he'd heard the ravens that belonged to his pack, but they hadn't cawed again.

He raced ahead of Tall Tailless, relishing the grass beneath his pads and the smell of prey streaming over his nose. He didn't care that they were making for the Great Hard Cold. The wind had turned and he could no longer hear the mountain's growls, or catch the stink of demons and burning rock.

In the distance Tall Tailless howled: *Where are you?*

Here! Wolf howled back. He could still see Tall Tailless wading through the grass, but his pack-brother's poor weak eyes could no longer see him.

A herd of reindeer barred his way. A stag put up its muzzle and bellowed, but the other reindeer saw that Wolf wasn't hunting and moved aside to let him through.

Again he caught the caws of ravens. His spirit leapt. Definitely the ravens who belonged to his pack!

Now the wind carried a sound he'd never heard before: a low rumbling, deeper than thunder – but gentle and slow, like the earth talking to itself.

Wolf heard that it was made of many voices, each full of feeling. He felt a pang, for these feelings were like those of his pack: playfulness, impatience, curiosity, love. He longed for his mate and cubs, and whined aloud.

But the rumblings came from creatures unknown, so Wolf slowed to a trot. He reached a wide Fast Wet with piles of dung on its banks. He smelt that the dung had been left by the unknown prey: prey so enormous that no wolf would dare hunt it alone. To hide his scent, he rolled in the dung till he was thoroughly caked.

He had to warn Tall Tailless, who'd fallen so far behind that Wolf couldn't see him. *Where are you?* he howled.

No answer. Only the Fast Wet tumbling over the rocks and the wind moaning in the grass.

TWENTY-FIVE

Where are you? howled Wolf.

Torak opened his mouth to howl back – then shut it. The riverbanks were high, he couldn't see over the top. Anything might be lurking on the other side: a musk-ox, an ice bear. A mammut.

All day he'd been heading upstream at a steady trot, but the ice mountain wasn't getting much closer and he'd lost sight of it, as the land was more hilly than he'd thought. Once he'd seen a snow owl watching him from an outcrop. *Don't let Naiginn hurt Renn,* he'd begged the guardian of the Far North. *I'll do anything you want, just don't let him hurt her.*

He came to a stretch where the river ran wide and shallow. The banks on the opposite side were rocky and steep, but on his side they were a gentle slope of willows and sedge. The shallows had been trampled by huge round feet. Torak made out the trails of several full-grown mammut and the smaller prints of a young one. The youngster had slipped as it climbed the slope, then hurried after the grown-ups.

The herd had flattened a broad swathe of sedge on its return to the plains, leaving mounds of greenish-brown droppings. They smelt like horse dung. Torak hoped this meant that mammuts didn't eat meat.

He found more droppings near a jumble of boulders that looked as if they'd been piled up by a flood. The droppings were steaming. Torak was examining them when he became aware of a faint, deep rumbling. It sounded like distant thunder and it was getting louder.

Taking cover among the boulders, he heard an answering rumble: as if two rocks were talking to each other. The rumblings came nearer. He heard slow huffings, croppings, munchings. Mist rose from the other side of his hiding-place.

Or was it breath?

In front of him a slab of basalt lay aslant another, with a clump of mushrooms beneath. A thick, furry brown snake reached under the slab and flipped it aside as easily as a blackbird overturning a leaf. The 'snake' ended in what looked like a wrinkled finger and thumb. These delicately plucked a mushroom, then coiled back and disappeared.

More rumbling and munching. Sweat trickled down Torak's spine.

Where are you? Wolf howled again.

Torak dared not reply. He was pretty sure there was a mammut on the other side of these rocks.

Again the trunk appeared. This time it snaked round and bumped his shoulder. The rumbling rose: *What's this?* Musky breath heated his face as the forked tip of the mammut's trunk probed his throat, his nose, his brow… It felt like warm, supple rawhide but it could twist off his ear as easily as it had plucked that mushroom. He stifled a cry as the finger and thumb grabbed a lock of his hair and tugged. The mammut let go and withdrew its trunk. Maybe it had decided he wasn't good to eat.

As he wiped the sweat from his face the sky darkened. Glancing up, he saw a shaggy brown mountain gazing down at him from the other side of his boulder.

The mammut was resting its tusks on top of the rock while it pondered this odd little creature below. Its domed head was a forest of nutbrown fur rising to another forested hump between its shoulders. Its rheumy gaze met Torak's, wise and unafraid. To the mammut he was no different from the teeming midges in the sedge: another brief life that would soon flicker and blink out.

At last the huge beast seemed to lose interest. It ambled towards the river, placing its tree-trunk feet so softly that all Torak heard was the swish of tusks through sedge and that sonorous rumbling, so full of mysterious feeling.

He watched it uproot a willow bush the size of a boar, cram it in its mouth and begin to chew. It went on chewing, occasionally flicking its short, tufted tail.

Torak was about to make his escape when three more mammuts appeared on the slope behind him. A grizzled old one waded stiffly into the shallows, where it sucked water through its trunk and sprayed its back with slit-eyed pleasure. A darker mammut with yellowish tusks found a patch of gravel, sat down and scratched its bottom. A buff-coloured giant approached the nutbrown one and they rumbled affectionately, lightly rubbing tusks and entwining trunks. Still more mammuts appeared. Torak was surrounded.

They were so shaggy it took him a while to work out that the old one was the only male. Maybe mammuts were like aurochs, and the females herded together, while males in their prime wandered alone until seized by the urge to mate.

Something told Torak that the nutbrown mammut was the leader of the herd. He remembered a mare in the Deep Forest who'd been leader of *her* herd. The nutbrown mammut showed the same vigilance, keeping an ever-watchful eye on her kin. Perhaps it was not by chance that she had found him first.

A high-pitched squeal rang out and a baby mammut tottered towards the nutbrown female. The calf was as big as a bison, but the milk-tusks poking through its blond fur were only as long as Torak's thumb. His heart sank as he watched it duck under its mother's belly to suckle. These giants might seem peaceable, but they would doubtless turn deadly in defence of their young.

And they showed no sign of leaving. To escape he would have to walk through the herd. A startled mammut might skewer him on its tusk, or break his back with a thwack of its trunk. It might simply tread on him by mistake.

The calf finished suckling and wandered off, dribbling milk. To Torak's horror it was coming towards him. Willing it to stay away, he shrank deeper among the boulders – but like all young creatures it was curious. It halted two paces from his hiding-place, blinking at him through long blond eyelashes.

'Shoo!' he whispered.

The calf stretched its trunk towards him and sniffed.

He waved his arms. *'Shoo!'*

He had no idea whether mammuts were clever, but this one wasn't. It went on staring, breathing noisily through its trunk.

Suddenly Wolf appeared on the bank on the other side of the river. Scrambling down the rocks, he splashed across and went for the youngster, snapping and snarling.

The nutbrown female moved at frightening speed to protect her calf. A swing of her trunk sent Wolf flying. He hit the ground with a yelp but was up in an instant, hurtling for the boulders to take refuge with Torak. The calf fled for the shallows and sank knee-deep in mud. Unable to get out, it burst into startled squeals. It didn't stop squealing till its mother hooked her trunk under its belly and hauled it to safety.

As she steered her calf towards the others, she eyed Torak irritably: *Stay away from my herd.*

Yes, but *how?* He was desperate to make a break for it, but the mammuts were going nowhere.

Beside him Wolf's hackles were bristling. He was snuffing the wind. Uff!

At that moment every single mammut stopped what it was doing and stared upriver. Their rumblings grew louder and they were flapping their ears: they were alarmed. Swiftly they surrounded the youngster, facing outwards to defend it from whatever threat they'd sensed.

At last Torak caught what Wolf and the mammuts had heard: furious bellows heading this way.

With an ear-splitting shriek the bull mammut rushed down the slope, nearly crashing into the boulders where Torak and Wolf were hiding – then veered round to attack the herd. Its tusks were longer than its body, extravagantly curved and brown at the tips, as if from savaging earth. Torak only glimpsed its eyes but that was enough: this wasn't the frenzy to find a mate. Something had sent this huge bull mad.

Rumbling loudly, the herd stood its ground while the bull gouged mud with its tusks and uprooted willows like grass, raising clouds of dust. Flinging up its trunk it uttered a bellow that shook the ground. It charged. The lead female rushed to meet it.

The clash of their foreheads was a thunderclap. They staggered back, charged again, tusks crashed and locked. The female was smaller but wily, twisting her head, taking the bull by surprise. One foot slipped. The female shoved the bull against the boulder behind which Torak and Wolf crouched. It rocked alarmingly, like a tooth working loose. If that happened again they'd be squashed like flies.

With an urgent glance at Torak, Wolf made a break for the river. Torak couldn't see for the dust. Trusting his pack-brother, he dashed past the herd.

The river was shallow yet strong, mud sucking his boots as he floundered across. The opposite bank was a wall of unclimbable rock.

'Torak!' yelled a voice. 'Over here!'

He faltered. That couldn't be *Renn?*

Behind him the bull rushed to head-slam the female. She dodged. One of the bull's tusks struck a boulder with shattering force, snapping off at the root. Shrieking in agony, the bull staggered into the river, shaking its ruined head and spattering Torak with blood.

'Here! Upstream!' screamed Renn.

Wolf had scrabbled to the top of the rocks but Torak couldn't find a way up. Wolf skittered down again, barking frantically at him to follow.

The wounded bull was lurching after Torak, blaming him for its agony.

'Torak, here!' A flash of red against black and there she was, halfway up a gully. 'Take my hand! I'll pull you up!'

'I'm too heavy, I'd drag you down!'

The bull was rampaging towards him. Torak spotted a handhold and swung himself off the ground, the bull's remaining tusk raking the basalt where he'd been an instant before.

Rearing on its hind legs, the great beast flung its trunk high to dash Torak off the gully – overbalanced, toppled backwards – and lay still.

TWENTY-SIX

'Where's Naiginn?' demanded Torak, gripping Renn's shoulders so fiercely she winced. 'Did he hurt you? Are you all right?'

'I'm fine!' she lied.

She saw him notice the marks on her neck, her burnt and bloodied feet. His eyes turned flinty. 'He did that.'

'I told you I'm all right. There's blood on your face—'

'Not mine, the mammut's. Where is he? Where's Naiginn?'

'I don't know but he can't be far, we've got to get out of sight! Come on, there's a thicket down there.'

A green slope fell steeply to a willow-fringed stream where Renn had been hiding when she'd heard the mammuts. Dusk was gathering under the trees. She watched Torak fling down his weapons and sleeping-sack and take in the marks of power she'd daubed on stones to ward off Naiginn.

'When did you last see him?' he said brusquely.

'Back near the coast.' Swiftly she told him how Naiginn had hunted her through the demon breath. 'I saw something coming. It was a mammut. He shot it with a poisoned arrow, that's what sent it mad. He can't be far, but if he was close, Rip and Rek would have warned us.'

Torak glanced at the ravens wheeling overhead.

Wolf was prowling the slope above the thicket. He hadn't come near them, and with a pang Renn realized why. 'Wolf's angry with me.'

Torak drew a waterskin from inside his parka and crouched by the stream to fill it. 'He doesn't understand why you left. It'll take him a while to trust you again.'

'What about you? Do you trust me?'

'...Of course I do.'

But she'd caught his hesitation. She sat on a boulder and clutched her knees to stop them shaking.

'How did you find me?' said Torak.

'I heard Wolf howling.' Plunging her feet in the icy water, she grabbed sedge and rubbed a blister on her heel. It hurt. Good, it was what she deserved. Because of her they were stuck on this horrible island and that mammut had nearly killed Torak—

'Renn, stop it!' He gripped her hands in his.

'I left you,' she said in a low voice.

'Yes, you did. Twice.'

'I thought I was saving you, but he made it all up!'

'You took my food too, don't forget that.' He was almost smiling. 'I'm not angry with *you*, I'm angry with *him*!'

'Are you sure?'

'Of course.'

She could see that he believed that. But words aren't feelings, and she wondered whether deep down in his heart, it was really true.

They ate some of Shamik's ptarmigan tongues and a few mushrooms they found upstream. Sunset soon, the sky glowing red.

Now that Renn had washed the grime off her face it had lost that stretched, hunted look which Torak found unbearable. As he watched her cutting a strip off the hem of her robe so that she could move more freely, he could almost believe that she was the same girl he had loved in the Forest.

They divided his weapons between them. He gave her his quiver and bow, and kept his slingshot, axe and slingstones. He wanted to give her his knife, but she said she could make one from some black flint and an antler she'd found by the stream.

'You'd better have my boots,' he said.

'Why should you go barefoot instead of me?'

'Because.' He was already stuffing them with fern fronds to make them fit. 'And I won't be barefoot, Tanugeak gave me salmon-skin socks. I can tie them on with what you've cut off your robe.'

'That won't work.'

'Yes, it will.' In the end he wore her down and she accepted his boots, although first he brought out his birch-bark cone of pine salve and she smeared some on her feet, while he did her neck and wrists. He was as gentle as he knew how, but she bit her lips in pain. In his mind he grabbed Naiginn by the hair and beat his handsome face to a pulp…

'I'm still hungry,' said Renn.

They agreed to save the rest of the ptarmigan tongues, and gathered more mushrooms and some lingonberries they found on the slope. Lingonberries were Wolf's favourites, but when Renn offered him a handful he gave her a hard stare and trotted away.

Rip and Rek stalked about hoping for scraps, then flew off to the fallen mammut on the other side of the ridge.

Renn asked Torak how he'd found the Island and he told her about spirit walking in the sea-eagle, and Marupai and Shamik. 'We got separated in the fog. If they made it ashore, they'll be on the other side of the ice mountain.'

They were silent. Then Torak said what they'd both been thinking. 'If you heard Wolf howling, so did Naiginn.'

She nodded. 'He'll know you're on the Island.'

'I think he wanted me here all the time.' He told her about the waymarkers Naiginn had left for him.

Again Renn's face became shadowed. 'He thinks he can make me do what he wants by threatening to hurt you. That's what he's done all along. He'll do it again.'

'He won't get the chance.'

'He's a demon, Torak. My mother put an ice demon in her child. Think what that means! He's utterly ruthless. And some of his arrows are poisoned.'

Torak remembered Naiginn's pale-blue eyes with their frozen black cores. 'Why didn't we see it sooner? My scar itching, and yours and Wolf's. Why couldn't we tell he's a demon?'

'My mother wove a masking spell to hide what he is. That's why he needs me. It's also a binding spell, it can only be broken in the ice cave where he was born and only by a Mage of his bone kin.' She was shaking her head. 'All summer he was watching us in the Forest. He tricked me into believing I wanted to hurt you – and I never sensed it! Fine Mage I turn out to be.'

'You were up against your mother's spell. She was one of the most powerful Mages who ever lived.'

Renn wasn't listening. 'That moment when he stopped pretending: when I saw what he really is… He hates all living creatures. To him we're merely *things*. If we get in his way—'

'He'll regret it.'

'No, Torak, listen! There's something you have to know. Marupai isn't his father. His real father was a Soul-Eater – from the Seal Clan.'

He looked at her.

'You know what that means,' she said. 'Your father's mother was Seal Clan, so he's not only *my* bone kin, he's yours. If you killed him you'd break one of our oldest laws—'

'I've broken other laws.'

'Not this one. Killing your bone kin means being cast out for ever. Not even Fin-Kedinn could speak to you. Not even me.'

She was right, but he didn't want to hear it. Springing to his feet, he prowled up and down. 'I won't need to kill him,' he said abruptly. 'We'll leave him here on the Island. Winter soon, he won't last long; not even if he is the best hunter in the Far North.' An unwelcome thought occurred to him. 'But how do *we* get away? My boat was smashed on the coast.'

'We'll take his. If we get to higher ground I think I can work out where he left it. Although he might guess that's where we'll go.'

'Good,' snarled Torak. 'How far to his boat?'

'Let's climb to those boulders upstream and take a look.'

The ice mountain was closer than Torak had thought. It glared at the crimson sky, stony hills lapping its feet like a black Sea.

Renn pointed east of the hills to a smoky charcoal plain. 'That's the way I came.'

Torak's hand tightened on his knife as he thought of Naiginn hunting her across that burning land. 'Let's go.'

'Not yet,' she said in an altered voice. She was staring back in the direction they'd come.

Torak saw the rocky bank he'd scrambled up to escape the mammut. The carcass of the great beast lay at the bottom, by the river. To his surprise, the herd had clustered around it, as if standing guard.

Renn was staring intently at the mammuts. Her face was still, her dark eyes opaque. Torak knew that look. It meant she was doing what Mages do: reading hidden patterns and signs.

'Renn?' he said quietly. 'Why can't we set off now?'

She came to herself and met his gaze. In the fierce red light her expression was resolute and defiant. 'Something I have to do first.'

TWENTY-SEVEN

The pack-sister had offered Wolf lingonberries but he'd ignored her. Did she think she could abandon Tall Tailless *twice*, then make it all right with *berries*?

She had split up the pack, she had forced them to follow her to this terrible place full of demons. If Wolf's mate had done that he would have grabbed her muzzle in his jaws, slammed her to the ground and *growled* till she said sorry.

But there'd been no muzzle-grabbing between Tall Tailless and his mate and she hadn't said sorry. They were arguing in tailless talk, Tall Tailless waving his forepaws, the pack-sister stubbornly shaking her head. Wolf left them to it and trotted up the ridge.

Down by the Fast Wet the long-noses were rumbling as they gathered round the carcass of the fallen one. They sounded sad, and Wolf smelt that the bull had been their brother. They were grieving just as deeply as wolves grieve for their own – but in a different way, stroking the body with tusks and trunks, touching its ears and eyes.

Wolf saw a dim, shaggy shadow rise from the carcass. It was the Walking Breath of the fallen bull, but it didn't yet know that it was no longer alive.

Awkwardly it raised its trunk and touched the cheek of the lead female. She didn't feel it. Wolf watched her wade into the wet where the bull's broken tusk lay. Wrapping her trunk around it, she carried the tusk to the carcass and laid it on top. Puzzled, Wolf saw other long-noses piling on willow and sedge.

The Hot Bright Eye went to sleep, the Dark came, and still the bull's Walking Breath stayed watching the herd. At last Wolf saw its head droop: it understood. Plodding across the Fast Wet, it glanced back for the final time, then sadly walked away.

Soon the herd also crossed the Fast Wet, and stood in the sedge and went to sleep. Their grief hung heavy in the air. Their togetherness reminded Wolf of his pack. He felt a howl begin, but he didn't let it out. His mate and cubs were too far away to hear.

The ravens were hopping about on the covered-up carcass. Unable to get at it, they cast hopeful glances at

Wolf: *Come and help!* Wolf was hungry, but the long-noses were too close. He'd seen how fast they could move.

Tall Tailless and the pack-sister came up behind him. Tall Tailless asked Wolf to stay and keep watch, but in a way that told Wolf that he didn't like what he was about to do. Then to Wolf's astonishment and alarm, Tall Tailless and the pack-sister began climbing down to the carcass.

'Hurry *up!*' whispered Torak, jerking his head at the slumbering herd.

The night wasn't dark, but Renn hesitated before the shadowy carcass. The herd had covered it completely, she couldn't tell which end was which.

Torak lifted a branch to expose a shaggy leg.

'No,' she muttered. 'It has to be the head.'

'Why? And why this mammut? Why can't we use hair snagged on rocks?'

'Because Naiginn shot this one, that's why.'

He moved to the broken-off tusk at the other end of the carcass and raised it with an effort. 'Head's under here...' Renn heard the strain in his voice.

Uff! warned Wolf from the top of the bank.

Across the river a mammut stood in the shallows, flapping its ears. Renn couldn't see its eyes but she felt its stare.

'*Hurry!*' whispered Torak, still raising the tusk.

Ducking underneath, she breathed the sickly-sweet smell of death. Her groping fingers touched a huge rough tongue, a jagged stump of tusk. She found the top of the domed head with its forest of coarse hair, grabbed a handful and hacked with Torak's knife.

'That's it, let's go!' he hissed.

'I need more!' She stuffed clumps down her front.

Chuk-chuk-chuk! echoed the ravens' warnings. Wolf was barking frantically. The entire herd was awake and splashing towards them.

Seizing Renn's arm, Torak ran for the gully. A bellow, terrifyingly close. Torak swung himself up, reached for her wrists and hoisted her to safety.

Panting, they lay side by side, listening to the mammuts' agitated rumbling below.

Torak glanced at Renn. 'Tell me you got enough hair.'

They burst into jittery laughter.

Back at the stream Renn said she had to burn the hair to ash – but Torak said no, fire was too risky.

'Just a few clumps of hair,' she protested. 'No one would see that.'

'Oh, no,' he said drily. 'Because burning hair doesn't make thick smoke you can spot three daywalks away.' But she didn't back down, so with a sigh he tossed her his tinder pouch.

He found a slab of basalt and she woke a spark on it with his strike-fire, then burnt the hair while he scattered the smoke with a bough. After grinding the ash to fine dark powder, she mixed half with earthblood, bloodstone and pine salve. Some of this paste she rubbed on Torak's forehead and breastbone; he did the same for her. He also smeared a little between Wolf's ears, where he couldn't lick it off.

'This is to protect us from demons, yes?' said Torak.

'Especially Naiginn. He doesn't like earthblood or bloodstone, but he's *frightened* of mammuts. He flinched when ash touched his boots.'

By now they were both exhausted, but Torak insisted on making Renn a knife by slotting her flint flake in a piece of antler. Having no pine-pitch for glue, he tied the blade in place with sinew from his sewing kit, wetting it first so that it would shrink tight as it dried. He was about to wind more sinew round the handle when Renn held out some strands of mammut hair. 'Use these.'

'I thought you'd burnt it all.'

'I kept some back. I've a feeling I'll need it.'

He handed her the finished knife.

'There's something else,' she said in a low voice. 'The riddle. I told you about the island of birds. And you found the forest in the treeless land.'

'Which leaves the third part: *Save the past by burning the present.*'

'At Waigo I had a vision. I saw the Deep Past: people hunting mammuts till there were none left. The mammuts on this island... They're the last of their kind. I don't know what the third part means, but I think "the past" means the mammuts.'

'But – the riddle is about finding what we seek, and I've found you, so why—'

'I don't think this is only about us, Torak. After I left the Forest I saw my mother in a dream. That couldn't have been one of Naiginn's tricks.'

He frowned. 'I just remembered something. The night Dark told me why you left, we saw the First Tree. It was pointing north. Naiginn couldn't have done that either. What does it mean?'

'I don't know. But whatever happens, I'll be ready.'

While they were talking, she'd sewn a pouch from the remains of Torak's headband. He watched her fill it with the rest of the powdered mammut ash, her face stern and determined.

He said, 'You think you're going to need that too.'

'I know I am.' She handed him back his sewing kit and yawned.

'When did you last sleep?'

'Can't remember. What about you?'

'Same.'

They were silent, thinking of Naiginn.

'The mammuts might keep him away,' said Renn.

'And Wolf will warn us, and Rip and Rek.'

They found a hollow under some boulders and turned it into a rough shelter with willow branches. Renn dragged in more springy armfuls and laid soft ferns on top, then Torak slit open his sleeping-sack to cover them both.

By the time he'd crawled in, Renn was whiffling in her sleep. Fitting his body around her, he buried his face in her hair. He could hear Rip and Rek preening in a nearby tree and Wolf snuffing the air. Feeling more at peace than he had since leaving the Forest, he tightened his arms around Renn.

He was resolving to stay awake and keep watch when he fell asleep.

'We've come too far west,' panted Renn. 'I don't remember this.'

Like Torak she was wearing her eyeshield, so he couldn't see her expression, but he heard the apprehension in her voice.

They'd set off after a brief unrefreshing sleep and had been climbing all day. They could feel the chill breath of the ice mountain, but this charred ravine hid it from view.

The rocks were treacherous with black ice, and Torak paused to strap on his 'raven claws'. It began to snow. Soon it was falling thick and fast. Wolf loped ahead and disappeared.

Torak caught the muted roar of water, which grew suddenly louder as they rounded a spur. The ice mountain towered over them, grey with rubble through the whirling snow. From a gash in its underbelly thundered a murky torrent.

'This feels bad!' Renn shouted above the roar.

'This stream heads east,' Torak shouted back. 'If we follow it we'll reach the coast. Can you find his boat from there?'

She wasn't listening, she was staring at the gash in the mountain's belly. Around it the ice was jagged and dark as rotten teeth, rocks and pebbles skittering down from above.

'The ice cave where Naiginn was made,' she yelled. 'He said there was another way in!'

'You think this is it?'

She nodded.

'Then we can't be far from the coast!'

'Maybe, but—' Her face changed. *'Behind you!'*

A hand wrenched Torak's arm violently up and over his head. His shoulder cracked, pain exploding, knocking him off his feet. As he struggled to his knees he heard Renn screaming his name. He saw Naiginn dragging her into the ice cave's rotten jaws.

The last thing Torak saw before he blacked out were those jaws crashing shut behind them.

TWENTY-EIGHT

The roof of the tunnel struck Renn a dizzying blow on the temple.

'Told you to duck,' snarled Naiginn. 'And this time no tricks.' Jerking the rope that bound her wrists, he dragged her deeper into the freezing, echoing gloom beneath the ice.

The tunnel dropped steeply, water streaming down its walls and over Renn's boots. She was soaked and shivering, the protective mammut ash washed off her skin. In her mind she saw Torak grey-faced on his knees, his right arm hanging useless at his side. 'What did you do to him?' she cried.

'Winged him,' said Naiginn. 'He'll be weak as a baby with one arm out of joint.'

'He'll still come after us.'

'So much the worse for him.'

'I'll never do what you say. I won't break the spell and set you free.'

'Then you'd better pray he doesn't find us because I'll cut the tendons behind his knees and cripple him for good.'

When she didn't reply he turned. His eyes were a frozen lightless blue. 'You have no choice but to do as I say. This Island is *mine*, it's helped me at every turn. The Sea washed Torak's boat past the coast so I knew where to find you. Just now the ice shut him out. With every step nearer the cave where I began, it's making me stronger!'

Deeper they went, and the din of water grew louder. Suddenly the tunnel opened out and Renn found herself in a vast, roaring cavern of otherworldly blue. Even the air burnt with cold blue fire. Overhead she saw hard clear waves of pallid blue in which pebbles, rocks, boulders hung suspended. Like them she was trapped.

Before her a shaft of hazy blue sunlight slanted through a hole from the world above – but that only deepened her sense of being cut off from the land of the living. The ice mountain creaked and groaned, she felt its weight pressing down on her. She glanced at her hands and they were livid, like those of a corpse.

From where she stood, the stream joined a torrent that spewed from the back of the cave over a rocky tongue and down to a spiked mouth that let in a sickly glimmer of daylight. Renn's teeth began to chatter. That was the same fanged maw she had seen from the Sea.

It might as well be on the moon. Naiginn had taken her weapons. The plan she'd thought up on reaching the Island would never work. What she'd dreaded had come true. The ice had swallowed her. She would never get out.

'This is where I began!' cried Naiginn, flinging his arms wide. 'Soon I will be free to prey on the living!' In the deathly glow his demon nature was revealed. Skin, hair, eyes: all were a raw, inhuman blue. Like Renn he was drenched, but he wasn't shivering. He revelled in the cold.

Dragging her to the edge of the torrent, he slung her over his shoulder and crossed from boulder to boulder, sure-footed in his element. The other side was a gravelly ledge a few paces wide. 'Here! Here you will break the spell!'

Around her rose spurs of clear ice, but deep at the back of the cave she caught an evil red glimmer. Her mind flew to her first sight of the Island, and the fiery glare on the smoky headlands flanking the ice mountain. Perhaps a tunnel led to some crack that opened on the Otherworld: a crack forever venting demons.

Through the echoing roar she made out voices as chill as splintered bone. Something slipped behind a spur. Above her the ice warped into a cruel face. With a cry she fell, and beneath her hands the ice moved, jaws gaped to bite. Demons slithered cackling into the gloom as Naiginn hauled her to her knees.

'See how they flock to honour me! It's time! Do what you must to break the spell!'

Demon laughter raked her ears, numbing her thoughts, draining courage. The ice would kill her as it had killed her father...

'I will submit,' she told Naiginn above the clamour. 'I will break the spell and set you free.'

'If you trick me I'll know it,' he said.

'I won't,' she lied. Her mother had done everything sideways like a snake: she had lived by deceit. Renn drew on that now.

They were on the ledge by the torrent, Naiginn squatting, intent on the spell, Renn shivering on her knees. 'Tell me what you're going to do,' he commanded.

'I told you before,' she said through chattering teeth. 'Our mother's m-masking spell binds your souls. To set you free I must become raven and p-peck it off.'

'Why raven? The worst tricksters of all!'

'This is the hardest M-Magecraft, so I need the power of the moon – and First Raven made the moon. Give me that kelp from the beach and the shell. And untie my hands.'

'Oh, no.'

'Do it! I can't break the spell if I'm bound.'

Reluctantly he obeyed. 'Tell me what it involves.'

From the neck of her robe she drew her duckbone whistle. 'First I call my spirit guides. Then I make my raven mask.

K-kelp for feathers. I'll paint them black with … octopus ink, sew them together with sinew. When I put on the mask you must be *silent* or it won't work.'

His eyes glittered. 'How long till I'm free?'

'As long as it takes. No more talk!'

Making him stay where he was, she withdrew a couple of paces till she'd put the shaft of blue sunlight between them. Behind her, the glimmer of the Otherworld. Ice fears fire. Demons fear the Otherworld. Naiginn avoided looking at it. That might prevent him seeing what she did.

Squatting, she put the whistle in her mouth and blew. *Find me, help me!* she called Wolf silently. If he heard, he would not let her down – but how could even Wolf hear through the voice of the torrent and the groans of the ice?

Bending to hide what she did, she smeared one side of the kelp fronds with dark mammut ash. With a bone needle and mammut hair, she threaded the short ends of the fronds in a row to make a long fringe of black 'feathers'. Next she smeared earthblood on the other side of the feathers, turning them red. Then she bit off a piece of hollow kelp stem to make a thumb-sized tube.

'Hurry!' shouted Naiginn.

She motioned him to silence.

A crash shook the ledge. Far below, a giant fang of ice had fallen from the mouth of the cave. The mountain was becoming angry, it knew what she meant to do.

Unseen talons tugged at her will. She sensed demons creeping up behind her: they knew she was about to

209

invoke their age-old foe. Doubts rushed in. Wolf wasn't coming. This wouldn't work, that great maw would snap shut, trapping her for ever...

Quork! Raven caws echoed down the column of blue daylight.

Uneasily, Naiginn stirred. Renn signed him to be still. 'My spirit guides are come!'

Fearing the ravens, the demons withdrew – and Renn's courage returned. Shutting her mind to all else, she took the moon-pale shell and tied it on her forehead with more mammut hair.

The instant the shell touched her brow she felt the moon's power coursing through her. In the dark of the Beginning, First Raven had brought light to the world by fetching the sun in his beak – but as he flew he'd dropped a chunk, which became the moon. The moon had always been special to Renn and she called on it now: *I have honoured you all my life. Help me become one with your great sister the sun.*

With trembling fingers she tied the kelp fringe around her brow so that its 'feathers' hid her face, their black sides outwards, the red against her skin. Crouching, concealed behind the feathers, she smeared her nose, cheeks and chin with earthblood. Lastly she scooped the remaining ash into the kelp-stem tube and gripped it between her front teeth.

In the distance she caught a new sound. *Was that Wolf?*

She couldn't wait a moment longer, she had to carry out her plan. Still with head down, she crawled towards Naiginn. When she reached the blue daylight she flung up her head and swept back the feathers, turning black to fiery red. At the same moment she blew a blinding cloud of mammut ash in Naiginn's face, then spat out the tube. 'Not raven but *sun!*' she shouted – and shoved him down the slope.

Howling, clawing his eyes, he tumbled over the rocks and disappeared into the murk. The ice creaked, another fang crashed, half-blocking the mouth of the cave. It was hopelessly far below, Renn had only moments to get there before it snapped shut.

As she sought a way down, she heard Wolf howling clear and strong. But how could this be? His howls weren't coming from the cave mouth below, they came from *behind*: from the evil red tunnel that led to the Otherworld.

TWENTY-NINE

Wolf howled for the pack-sister, but her singing bone didn't call again. The wind carried Tall Tailless's desperate cries over the Great Hard Cold as he dropped further behind, clutching his injured forepaw to his chest: *Go! Find the pack-sister!*

At last Wolf reached the edge of the Great Hard Cold. It fell to a smoky black plain and he caught the nose-biting stink that frightened off other smells. He heard the far-off bellow of a long-nose and the clatter of demon claws.

The pack-sister had been dragged under the Great Hard Cold by the bad tailless who'd hidden his demon souls so cunningly that not even Wolf had sensed what he was. Wolf had to find her. It didn't matter that she'd left

Tall Tailless, she and Tall Tailless were one, just as Wolf and his mate were one.

Picking his way down to the plain, Wolf spotted a demon slithering into the smoke. He smelt others, he ached to give chase – hunting demons was what he was for – but he had to find the pack-sister. *And* he had to protect Tall Tailless. Wolf didn't know what to do.

Again he caught the song of the pack-sister's singing bone, clear and high above the growls of the Great Hard Cold. He howled back: *Where are you?*

No answer.

Wolf heard a noise that made his pelt tighten with fear: the deep crackling roar of a Bright Beast-that-Bites-Hot. A Bright Beast so huge it could swallow him in one gulp.

It sounded terrifyingly close, but he couldn't *see* it. Muzzle to the ground, he cast about, rock crunching under his paws, the Bright Beast's clamour biting his ears. *Where was it?*

Then, many lopes away, Wolf saw the earth crack apart and a Bright Beast shoot from within to attack the Up. Out of the crack slipped a demon, dark against the glare. Now the shadowy bulk of a long-nose was chasing it. The demon fled shrieking. Wolf took courage. He was not alone against the demons, the long-noses were hunting them too.

The ravens were cawing eagerly, swooping over the Great Hard Cold: they had found the pack-sister!

But as Wolf loped towards them, the ground grew hot beneath his paws — and in a snap he knew: the Bright Beast-that-Bites-Hot was *underneath*. This whole plain was a thin skin over a vast, angry Bright Beast that was fighting to get out.

Torak slipped and fell, jarring his injured shoulder. Biting back a scream, he waited for the agony to subside. Slid his good hand inside his parka, touched the bulge where his arm had been yanked out of the socket. Tried to push it back in. No good. He struggled to his knees.

Crossing the ice mountain would have been impossible without Tanugeak's raven claws strapped to his feet. With them it was almost impossible. He envied Wolf, who'd raced ahead, sure-footed on the ice — and whose black-ringed eyes didn't need an eyeshield that restricted vision.

Before him lay ridge after ridge of glaring blue, darkened in places by the menacing slash of a crevasse. Blue ice is the hardest: Torak knew that now. He'd tried using his axe as a pick but it simply bounced off.

Cresting the next ridge, he came to a sudden halt. Before him a sheer drop to a fathomless blue void. From within came the echoing thunder of water: one more step and he would have fallen in. Nothing could have saved him, he would have been swept to his death.

Sinking to his knees, he half-slid, half-crawled sideways along the ridge until he'd left the void behind. His breath came in painful gasps. His sweat ran cold.

He sensed rather than saw a demon slink out of sight. He turned. Nothing there. But he felt it.

He became uneasily aware of how much noise he made – his creaking clothes, his panting breath. Anything could be creeping up behind him.

Again he fell. This was hopeless. How could he save Renn when he could barely save himself? He would never get off the ice mountain. He was going to die out here.

He howled to Wolf: *Help the pack-sister! I can't go on! I can't!*

The ice flung back his despair: *I can't – I can't...*

Picturing Naiginn's handsome, arrogant face, he flushed with shame. 'Hopeless,' he muttered. 'Stupid, *weak*.' Even if he did make it off the ice mountain – even if he found Naiginn – how could he fight with only one arm?

A demon cackled.

'Get away from me!' yelled Torak.

Anger cleared his mind. Why was he lugging all this gear? Painfully he eased his sleeping-sack off his back. Now his weapons: which to discard? He would keep his axe and knife, but his slingshot was useless, he needed both hands to shoot.

Although – as a *sling* it would be perfect, the pouch could support his forearm.

215

Knotting the two ends with fingers and teeth hurt so much that he nearly blacked out, but somehow he did it, then manoeuvred the sling over his head. Much better. His injured arm lay secure against his chest, leaving his good arm free.

He realized that he still had his slingstones tied around his waist in a slipknot. At a tug they'd be ready to use, and he could throw as well with his left hand as his right.

If he managed to find his way off the ice, and *if* he found Naiginn – if, if, if – he would only get a single shot.

Well, then, he would make it count.

Torak's luck had changed. It started snowing, which reduced the glare: tearing off his eyeshield, he stuffed it inside his parka. Now he could see all around.

The snow also made it easier to track Wolf, who'd chosen a way that even his one-handed pack-brother could manage. At last Torak caught the rotten-egg whiff of bloodstone. Dirty smoke blew in his face, vicious as a kick in the head. He didn't care. He had reached the edge of the ice mountain.

Wolf was howling: *Pack-sister!* Torak caught the eager caws of ravens. It was Rip and Rek. Had they found Renn?

Through the smoke and the snow Torak saw charred plains of rippling rock that looked as if enormous fingers had raked them in furrows. Distant flares of fiery orange: the Otherworld bursting through. He thought of the burning plain on the other side of the mountain where Renn had fled from Naiginn. These must be the plains on the *other* side that he'd glimpsed from his skinboat.

Thanks to Wolf's trail, it didn't take him long to find his way off the mountain. Soon he was standing on rock – warm with the Otherworld's unclean heat – but *rock*, not treacherous ice.

To his left the edge of the ice marched into the haze: he guessed the Sea lay beyond. If he followed that edge, he might find another way into the cave where Naiginn had dragged Renn – or even the great fanged maw he'd seen from the boat.

To his right he spotted Wolf on a low ridge, fighting something he couldn't see. Wolf was leaping, snapping, worrying the unseen thing in his jaws. With a vicious shake he tossed it into the smoke. No sooner had he bounded off the ridge than it swelled like a rocky blister and split, spurting dazzling fountains of liquid fire.

Torak realized that this entire plain was a brittle burnt skin over the Otherworld. He wondered where the next blister would burst.

Wolf was loping over the plain, but he wasn't making for Torak, he was racing towards a hole at the ice edge some distance ahead. Rip and Rek were wheeling above it.

As Torak started forwards he saw Renn crawl out and struggle grimly to her feet. Her cheeks were streaked with earthblood. A white eye flashed on her brow. She spotted Torak and her face lit up.

'Don't move!' shouted a voice.

Twenty paces to Torak's right, Naiginn emerged from behind an outcrop with an arrow nocked to his bow. 'Renn, come here!' he ordered. 'Do it now or I will shoot Torak!'

THIRTY

Renn saw Torak thirty paces ahead through the whirling snow: swaying, clutching his shoulder. She saw Naiginn standing on the plain with an arrow aimed at Torak's chest. Naiginn was blinking furiously, but even half-blinded by mammut ash he could make that shot. 'Renn, come to me now!' he shouted. 'I'll shoot him if you don't!'

'Ignore him!' yelled Torak. 'Get under cover!'

'I can't, he'll kill you!' she cried. Then to Naiginn: 'Don't shoot, I'll come!'

Wolf streaked towards the boulders where Naiginn stood, legs braced, ready to shoot. As Wolf sprang, Naiginn swung round and let fly. Wolf yelped, twisted in mid-air and fell with an arrow in his haunch.

Before Torak could stagger to his aid, Wolf was on his

feet. With fangs bared he launched another attack, but Naiginn had climbed out of reach. Wolf leapt, fell back, leapt again. Perched in the rocks, Naiginn nocked another arrow to his bow. 'Stay back, Torak!' he warned. 'This one's poisoned! One more step and you'll watch your wolf die!' To Renn: 'Come here or I will kill them both!'

Renn saw Torak sink to his knees. Snow speckled his hair and shoulders. He looked hollow-eyed and spent.

With his good hand he wrenched his axe and knife from his belt and cast them away. 'Do as he says, Renn. It's over.'

The Long Claw-that-Flies had sunk deep in Wolf's rump. He snapped but couldn't pull it out. The pale-pelted demon was out of reach, barking at the pack-sister and aiming another Long Claw at Tall Tailless.

Tall Tailless was clutching his injured forepaw. Wolf saw a demon sneak towards him, flickering in and out of sight like a shadow under a wind-tossed tree. Wolf forgot the Long Claw and flew at it. The demon fled. Wolf's paws scarcely touched the rocks as he chased it over the plain, leaping blazing cracks and braving waves of muzzle-biting smoke.

The demon was fast, but Wolf was faster. He was within a snap of his prey when a long-nose emerged from the haze. As Wolf scrambled out of its way, the great beast gored the demon on the point of its tusk and flung it high.

The demon flew shrieking through the Up and hit the ground with a thud. Bellowing, the long-nose stomped on it with one tree-trunk foot. It went on trampling, grinding, crushing even the rocks in its fury, forcing the demon back where it belonged. Then with a toss of its head and a fierce glance at Wolf, it vanished into the smoke.

Pain sank its teeth into Wolf's rump and his hind leg began to shake. Again he snapped at the Long Claw, again he couldn't pull it out.

The Bright Soft Cold was no longer falling from the Up. Above the voices of the wind and the Bright Beast, Wolf heard the taillesses shouting. They were many, many lopes away. Wolf started limping towards them.

He hadn't gone far when he heard his pack-brother barking. But Tall Tailless wasn't calling for help. *Stay away, pack-brother!* he barked urgently. *This prey is* mine!

Torak had seemed full of resolve when he was barking at Wolf, but now as he turned back to Renn his shoulders slumped and he looked utterly defeated. 'Do as Naiginn says!' he told her again. 'It's over for me, but he needs you, he'll keep you alive!'

She couldn't believe it. Torak would never give up.

She *didn't* believe it. She saw the slingstones on the ground at his side. Through the last flakes of drifting snow their eyes met – and she understood. He couldn't see Naiginn hiding among the rocks, he needed to get him into the open, to have a clear shot.

Thirty paces to her left, across a rippling expanse of charred rock, Naiginn crouched on a boulder with an arrow aimed at Torak.

'Don't shoot!' Renn shouted. 'I will obey, I'm coming to you right now!'

She had to get him down from there, into the open. Cudgelling her brains, she started towards him.

A short distance to her right, a crack zigzagged across a rocky mound. The mound seemed to judder and swell, as if something were fighting to get out.

Suddenly Renn knew what to do.

'I will obey!' Renn shouted to Naiginn – but to Torak's horror, instead of heading for Naiginn's hiding-place, she ran onto a low mound that was cracking and shaking to life.

'Get off, it's going to blow up!' shouted Torak, frantically waving his good arm.

'Get away from there!' shrieked Naiginn.

'Make me!' Renn yelled back. 'I'm your last chance of freedom! If I die you'll be trapped for ever! Come and get me!'

The sun was a huge red globe in the smoky black sky, turning her hair to flame, flashing fire off the third eye on her brow. At any moment the Otherworld might erupt, yet she stood her ground to decoy Naiginn into the open.

Jumping down from the boulders, he ran towards her. The mound heaved. Still Renn stood firm – but Naiginn drew back in terror of the Otherworld beneath.

Torak seized his chance. Rising to his feet, he whirled the slingstones once, and threw with all his strength. Naiginn didn't see, his gaze was fixed on Renn. As she leapt off the mound the Otherworld broke through, crimson flames shooting high. A spark caught the slingstones in mid-air, they burst into flames. Naiginn screamed as the blazing missiles whipped round his throat. 'You put a leash on her!' roared Torak. 'I've done the same to you!'

Still screaming, Naiginn staggered through the smoke. Torak lost sight of him as the mound ruptured, spurting liquid fire like a severed vein. Hotter than the sun, it blazed glaring orange, spattering rocks, turning black smoke red.

'Renn! Where are you? *Renn!*' With his good arm Torak shielded his eyes, but the heat was beating him back.

Through the crimson smoke he caught the distant bellow of a mammut – then Naiginn's screams, abruptly cut off – but no Renn.

Torak's knees buckled.

As he struggled upright he saw Wolf limping out of the smoke and Renn running towards him over the rocks.

THIRTY-ONE

Now what? thought Renn.

Flames lit the night sky. The ice mountain was juddering, chunks crashing off it, the ground shaking beneath her feet. They had to get away before this end of the Island broke apart. But how? Torak was ashen-faced, Wolf had an arrow in his rump. The wind off the ice was freezing, and Renn was soaked from the cave and cold beyond shivering.

'It's not cold that kills, it's wet,' scolded Inuktiluk.

Inuktiluk? How did he get here? Sounds faded in and out. She couldn't keep her eyes open.

Torak was shaking her. 'Renn!'

'Go 'way,' she mumbled. 'I need to lie down.'

'If you fall asleep now you'll never wake up!'

224

She scowled. 'Who's that?'

A girl was running towards them through the smoke: small, with a withered arm and a determined expression.

Wolf was swinging his tail and limping towards her. Torak was waving his good arm. 'Shamik! Where's your boat?'

Never in his life had Torak experienced anything like it.

Snowflakes were settling on his face and on his clothes on the riverbank – and yet he was floating in blissful heat. He could feel the steaming water unravelling his knotted muscles, washing away the pain in his shoulder...

'Stay in a long time,' Shamik had told him. 'It'll be easier to pull your arm back in place.'

She'd taken charge with surprising firmness and led them to Marupai's skinboat on the shore. Skilfully she'd removed the arrow from Wolf's rump, then they'd piled into the boat and she'd paddled away from the burning chaos of the Island.

Torak had gazed in fascination at billowing black clouds ablaze with orange fire. Beside him Wolf had sat very still, and in his eyes Torak had seen a crimson light and tiny demons twisting like cinders. Then Wolf had rubbed his muzzle against Torak's cheek, and they'd watched the Island at the Edge of the World slipping away into the smoke.

Shamik had found a smaller island and put in for the night.

She'd pitched camp in a cave and woken a driftwood fire, helped Renn out of her wet clothes and into a sleeping-sack, and brought Torak to this steaming river that smelt faintly of bloodstone.

Upstream the water was too hot to touch, and dead trout floated belly up – but this pool was *perfect*, overhung with ferns and mint that made a fragrant pillow for his head. Drowsily he watched Shamik gathering ready-boiled fish for nightmeal. Wolf was on the shore, wade-herding live ones.

Slitting his eyes, Torak watched snowflakes spiralling towards him through the deep blue dusk. To the north the sky glowed red. His clothes on the bank were sprinkled with black ash. He thought of the mammut's bellow and Naiginn's last cry.

Marupai had also died on the Island. 'He went to help Naiginn,' Shamik had told them. 'I saw an ice spur fall on him. He knew he was going to die. When we went ashore he made me put Death Marks on him, and he gave me his map and his flute.'

Torak hoped the old man's souls were at peace. Blinded by love for a woman who'd wrecked his life, he had died believing that Naiginn was his son, the bravest hunter in the Far North. As for Shamik, it was hard to know what she thought of her newfound freedom.

'Wake up,' Renn said quietly in his ear. She was kneeling in the ferns, wearing his parka.

'I thought you were asleep,' he said.

She smiled. 'I came to find you before you drowned.'
He got out of the pool and she helped him rub himself dry
with snow and put on his leggings; then she told him to lie
on a flat-topped boulder she'd spread with ferns.

'Why?' he asked.

'Just do as I say. Lie face down with your bad arm over
the edge.'

Too drowsy to argue, he obeyed, and before he knew
it she'd gripped his arm and yanked it back in place with
a click and an eye-watering stab of pain. 'There,' she said.

'You could've warned me.'

'You'd have tensed up. Come on, let's get some sleep.'

At the cave they found Wolf sprawled by the fire, so full
of fish he merely thumped his tail. Shamik had dragged in
armfuls of dryish seaweed and piled rocks behind the fire
to throw the heat inside. Torak and Renn dug themselves
a nest, but Shamik insisted they take her sleeping-sack,
which she'd opened out for them, while she curled up in
the shadows at the back.

'How's your shoulder?' Renn mumbled against Torak's
chest.

'Not too bad.'

'You smell different.'

'So do you.' He blew a speck of ash off her hair.
Firelight danced on the roof of the cave. We're safe, he
told himself. But as he tumbled into sleep he thought,
We're still at the Edge of the World. How do we find our
way back?

The snow blew away in the night, but autumn had arrived. A hard frost had transformed the island from green to amber, with splashes of red like gouts of blood.

It turned out that Shamik could read Marupai's knot map, and with a strong wind behind them it didn't take long to reach Waigo. Wolf scarcely limped as he bounded off to the fells.

The Sea had thrown a huge shoal of tiny silver fish onto the shore below the Narwal settlement, and the whole clan was knee-deep in the bounty, raking it into seal-hide sacks. Because Torak and Renn arrived soon after the fish, the elders assumed they'd brought the good luck and treated them with honour. Orvo, who'd returned from the clan meet, helped translate. The elders seemed unmoved when Torak told them Marupai was dead, and asked no questions when he said Naiginn had gone hunting.

Next morning the Narwals equipped them for the journey south with boots, sleeping-sacks, smoked walrus and weapons for Torak – although they ignored Renn's plea for leggings and a bow.

'You should give your mate a good beating,' Orvo told Torak indignantly. 'Whoever heard of a half-man with a bow?'

Renn laughed. 'Doesn't matter, I'll steal Torak's.'

Torak grinned. Orvo looked astonished; then slightly wistful.

He walked with them to the skinboat. Torak's arm was back in its sling as his shoulder still hurt, and climbing in, he clenched his teeth. Orvo noticed. 'For a Softbelly you're not so soft,' he said with grudging respect. 'May the guardian swim with you.'

Torak smiled wryly. 'And also with you, my friend.'

There was just room in the boat for the four of them: Torak, Wolf, Renn and Shamik. The Narwals had 'given' her to Torak, but when he'd told her she was free she'd been confused. 'You don't want me to come?'

'Of course I do.'

'You saved our lives,' said Renn.

'But in the Forest we don't own people.' Torak wasn't sure if Shamik understood.

They set off down the coast, Renn and Shamik paddling, Torak grumbling at being unable to help. Wolf was restless, twice nearly capsizing them by turning round and refusing to sit.

Nights lengthened fast as they headed south. Dawns glowed a strange vivid purple, sunsets turned the sky to blood. One morning they woke to find the fells blanketed in snow.

The bird cliffs were deserted. Huge flocks of ducks and geese were gathering in the bays before flying south. Soon the World Spirit would change from a man with the antlers of a stag to a woman with bare red willow branches for hair. She would stride the land, breathing snow and hail, freezing lakes and stilling rivers and waterfalls with a touch of her hand.

The shallows were slushy with ice, and Torak saw his own concern in Renn's eyes. Once the Sea froze, they'd have to abandon the boat and trudge overland for days.

They passed the Three Peaks and spent a fraught morning dodging icebergs at the mouth of the ice river. Soon afterwards Wolf jumped to his feet, nearly capsizing them again. Torak growled, but Wolf's ears were pricked and his tail was high.

'What is it?' said Renn.

Torak broke into a grin. 'I think our journey just got easier. Look!'

He pointed at the shore, where a beaming Inuktiluk and his son were pulling up their dog sleds and shouting their names.

Inuktiluk put Shamik and the skinboat on his son's sled, and Torak and Renn went with him. Wolf had disappeared, overjoyed at feeling snow beneath his paws.

Nestled in reindeer skins, Torak and Renn listened to the patter of the dogs' paws and the scrape of whale-jaw runners. A snow owl flew past and Torak met its fierce yellow eyes. He had an odd sense that the guardian of the Far North wanted something.

Much later, lights glowed golden in the blue dusk and they slewed to a halt before the humped shelters of the White Fox Clan. After beating the frost from their clothes, they crawled into an orange fug of burning blubber and a noisy welcome. They were soon asleep in a warm eiderdown nest.

Torak woke to find Renn gone. She was sitting with Tanugeak by the blubber lamp. 'Come,' whispered Inuktiluk in his ear.

'I've told them about Nai— the ice demon,' Renn said quietly as Torak sat beside her. She'd corrected herself just in time; clan law forbids naming the dead for five summers.

Inuktiluk was shaking his head. 'If anyone else had told me, I wouldn't have believed it.'

'Nor I,' murmured Tanugeak. To Renn: 'But why do you feel to blame?'

'Because he tricked me! This whole journey has been for nothing!'

'Who can say what will flow from it?' the White Fox Mage said calmly. 'Torak, it's time to take off that sling. It'll hurt, but you need to start moving your arm. Renn tells me you spirit walked in an eagle. Tomorrow I'll do a rite to appease the north wind.'

To everyone's surprise, Renn said she would do it instead.

Tanugeak looked at her. 'At the clan meet you told me you hadn't done Magecraft for two summers. What's changed?'

Renn flushed. 'Me.'

Tanugeak's plump face dimpled. 'Then it wasn't for nothing, was it?' From under her cloak she drew Marupai's knot map and his flute. 'Shamik gave me these. Renn, you take the flute. It's mammut bone, keep it safe. Torak, you take the map. Think carefully what to do with it.'

Torak fingered the knotted mammut hair. He remembered the wise eyes of the lead mammut; her trunk gently stroking her fallen kin. He said, 'Renn had a vision of hunters killing them.'

'Our ancestors were greedy,' said Inuktiluk. 'They broke faith with the prey. It was a great evil.'

'I'm the last spirit walker,' Torak said thoughtfully. 'The mammuts on the Island are the last of their kind. I can't read this map, but Shamik can. Does that mean the Narwals can too?'

'Yes,' said Inuktiluk. 'And the Walruses and Ptarmigans, and some of us White Foxes.'

'Then while it exists,' said Torak, 'others could find the Island. They could hunt the mammuts.' He paused. 'If all the mammuts were gone, the fight against evil would be harder.'

Renn gasped. 'The last part of the riddle! *Save the past by burning the present.*'

He nodded. As he fed the map to the blubber lamp, the mammut hair crackled and smoked. 'Let them live out their lives in peace, untroubled by men.'

Renn kissed his jaw.

'What was that for?'

'For being the opposite of the ice demon.'

He snorted. 'Who was the handsomest man you ever saw.'

'Who never knew or cared how another living creature felt.'

Later as he drifted to sleep, he wondered if destroying the map was what the snow owl had wanted. Next morning he found a white wing-feather in the snow. Renn tied it to the back of his parka. 'A good sign,' she said.

They spent two days at the White Fox camp. Renn appeased the north wind by giving it Torak's greenstone wrist-guard, which she incised with his Forest sign and smeared with a few drops of his blood. Inuktiluk gave Torak a new wrist-guard of polished antler shaped like an eagle with outspread wings, and Renn a bow and a quiverful of arrows. Tanugeak gave her the longed-for parka and leggings, then astonished Shamik by giving her a set too. Renn fed their Narwal robes to the dogs.

That night the snow froze hard. This made a better surface for the sled-dogs, and Inuktiluk chuckled. 'The Far North wants you gone, my friends!'

The sleds sped off in the violet dawn, and on the third day they had come so far south that the Sea was clear, so they said goodbye to Inuktiluk and the dogs and continued in the skinboat, with Wolf following on land.

It had been the end of the Cloudberry Moon when they'd left the Forest, and though it felt longer, Torak and Renn had been surprised to learn from the White Foxes that they'd only been away for a little over a moon. The Moon of Green Ashseed had been and gone while they were in the Far North, although the White Foxes knew it by a different name.

Pausing with her paddle across her knees, Renn said, 'I can't understand how it can be the start of winter in the Far North, but the beginning of autumn in the Forest.'

'I know,' said Torak. 'When we get there it'll be the Moon of Roaring Stags.'

'What's a stag?' said Shamik.

'Like a reindeer,' said Renn. 'But bigger and not as shaggy.'

Shamik's face creased with worry: all these strange Forest creatures she didn't know.

'Dark will help you,' said Torak. 'He had to learn its ways too. He'd never seen horses or badgers—'

'Or hazelnuts,' said Renn. 'And *honey*! Wait till you taste honey!'

The snow was turning patchy, the fells dotted with green firs, crimson willows and yellow birch. As they paddled towards a headland, a south wind carried the scent of pines. Torak heard Rip and Rek cawing excitedly. The ravens were sky-dancing beak to tail. Torak saw a white flash flying with them.

Shamik's eyes widened. 'That raven's *white*!'

'It's Ark!' cried Renn.

With a whoop Torak threw up his axe and caught it one-handed. Then the skinboat cleared the headland and there was the Forest welcoming them home with wide green arms. Torak felt it filling his spirit like spring-water and he laughed aloud, drinking in the sight of dark pines and amber beeches, golden larches and scarlet rowans. He heard his pack-brother's delirious yelps echoing from the hills, then he spotted Fin-Kedinn and Dark hailing them from the shore, and behind them Wolf was hurtling through the trees – and a noisy torrent of happy wolves was plunging down the slope to greet him.

THIRTY-TWO

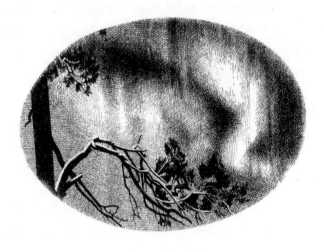

'What's wrong with Shamik?' Renn asked Dark as she oiled her new bow.

'Oh, some boys tricked her into sitting on a wood-ants' nest. They did that to me when I was new.'

'Is she all right?'

'She will be, I sent her off to pick juniper berries.' Turning a piece of bone in his long pale fingers, he studied it intently. 'Where's Torak?'

'On the ridge with Fin-Kedinn. How do you decide what you're going to carve?'

'I don't. I look at this bone and I say, "What's inside you?" and it tells me. "Ah!" I say. "So that's what you are!"' He smiled at her through his cobwebby white hair.

'So what's it telling you?'

'It's going to be a seal.'

They'd been back in the Forest for over a moon. Shamik had chosen to live with the Raven Clan and now followed Dark like a shadow. Renn and Torak were camped in the next valley, which was as near as they could get and still be with the wolves.

It had been the best autumn anyone could remember. The Ravens had gathered sacks of acorns and hazelnuts, and the cubs had eaten so many blackberries their muzzles turned purple. Torak's shoulder had healed. So had the burns on Renn's feet.

She was still trying to make friends with her new bow. Made of driftwood and whale bone bound with walrus sinew, it was shorter and stiffer than she liked. She was keener on her White Fox arrows, which were tipped with black flint and fletched with snow owl feathers for silent flight.

'Did you see that green ring around the moon last night?' said Dark.

She nodded.

'Someone in the Boar Clan saw a long-tailed star. Bad weather on the way, I think.'

'My smoke-reading told me the same thing. And Torak says Wolf sensed something bad coming from the Up.'

Frowning, Dark fingered the mammut-hair wristband she'd given him. Tanugeak had given it to her with a supply of mammut ash in a gutskin pouch. This made Renn faintly uneasy. Why had Tanugeak felt she needed it? What did she fear was coming?

Dark had resumed carving. The seal lifted its tiny snout as it powered through an invisible Sea, and Dark was cleverly using the bone's blotchiness to suggest mottled hide.

Renn said, 'Do you really think it's just bad weather on the way?'

'I'm not sure. But I'm glad you and Torak aren't camped far off. I think it's going to be a tough winter.'

'Yes,' said Renn. 'Yes, that must be it.'

Fin-Kedinn had asked Torak to help him dig pitfalls on the ridge.

After digging three, they'd moved further along and were setting snares. To mask their scent from the prey, they rubbed their hands with juniper berries from a bush near the hares' run, and handled the horsehair twine as little as possible. They took stakes from the same bush and smeared the cut ends with mud.

With a twinge of concern, Torak noticed that Fin-Kedinn's limp was worse, the lines at the sides of his mouth more deeply etched. Torak said, 'We don't have to do any more today.'

Fin-Kedinn nodded, but went on trimming a stake.

It was the Blackthorn Moon, when yellow birch leaves light up the Forest floor like little suns. In the mornings the valleys were filled with mist, and spiders' webs glittered in the bracken. Squirrels were busy hoarding food, while boars, jays and woodpigeons were simply enjoying the feast.

After the Moon of Red Willow the sun would go to sleep in its cave and it would be the Moon of Long Dark. Torak liked winter. Tracking was easier in snow, and he liked the feel of the sleeping Forest, when only firs and pines remained awake.

Fin-Kedinn planted the stake and positioned the horsehair loop. 'The signs are it'll be a hard winter.'

'Looks like it,' said Torak.

His foster father rose, leaning on his staff, and fixed him with his vivid blue gaze. 'Best if you and Renn stay close to the clan. Yes?'

Torak blinked. 'You think it'll be that bad?'

'I don't know. But I'd prefer you to stay close.'

To his surprise, Torak discovered that he no longer minded how close they camped to the Ravens. The arguments he used to have with Renn now seemed trivial. What did it matter where they camped? What mattered was that they were together.

He nodded. 'Yes,' he said. 'I think that would be best.'

Torak wasn't back when Renn returned to camp, so she went into their shelter and took a nap.

She woke some time later. It wasn't quite dusk and the wolves were still asleep. Wolf lay snoring beside a mound of slumbering cubs. Renn stepped over a well-chewed bone and trod on Darkfur's paw by mistake; they exchanged mute apologies.

A grey owl was roosting in an oak tree at the edge of camp. Cross-legged on the same branch sat Seshru the Viper Mage.

'You,' Renn said blankly.

Her mother's beautiful black mouth curved in a smile. 'Me.'

This time, Renn knew she was dreaming. But she didn't know how to wake up.

Seshru's hair was a river of darkness. The pupils of her eyes were vertical slits, like those of a snake. 'You've been doing Magecraft,' she mocked. 'Can this mean you've accepted that we're not so very different?'

'No,' said Renn. 'I have your marrow, I can't change that. How I use my skill is up to me.'

With fluid grace Seshru unwound herself and slid down to a lower branch that brought her face to face with Renn. 'But you still tell lies.' Her gaze flicked upwards, and a viper slithered down the trunk and coiled around her shoulders. 'You lied to the Narwals about your brother.'

'Half-brother.'

'You told them he'd gone hunting.'

'I couldn't tell them he'd died. And they'd never have believed us if we'd told them he was an ice demon.'

'How do you know he died? You never saw the body.'

'He was trampled by a mammut. We heard it.'

Seshru laughed. 'You didn't see it!' Plucking the viper from her throat, she drew her knife and languidly sliced it in two.

'But he's dead, I know he is!'

Both ends of the snake were wriggling, flecking Seshru's beautiful face with blood. Now they were *two* vipers. Smiling, she chopped them in pieces, which also became snakes: a seething, hissing mass rising and whirling around her. 'I told you before,' she said, laughing. *'It isn't over!'*

Her laughter was ringing in Renn's ears when she woke up.

She found Torak and Fin-Kedinn coming down the ridge. They hadn't seen her, and as she watched them walking gravely side by side her heart tightened with love and worry for them both.

The encounter with her mother had left her shaken. She couldn't work out what it meant.

If it means anything, she reminded herself. If it isn't merely another of her tricks.

She decided to say nothing about it to Torak. When they'd left the Far North she had promised herself that she would have no more secrets from him – but this was different. The Viper Mage was dead. So was Naiginn. She wouldn't *let* Seshru poison their lives with lies.

The following afternoon Torak lifted a corner of the firepit to see if the roe buck was cooked. Not yet.

That morning he and Renn had dug a trench and lined it with stones, piled it with logs and woken a fire. Once the embers had collapsed to ash, they'd dug them out and laid the carcass on the bed of hot stones, piling more hot stones on top, followed by juniper branches and mud.

While Renn was off gathering mushrooms, Torak had scraped the buck's skin and hung it on a branch out of reach of the wolves. He'd washed the guts and stuffed them with a mix of blood, fat, chopped heart and liver, then tucked the sausages into the firepit. Tomorrow they would share what was left with the Ravens.

Dusk fell. Torak woke another fire and sat down to wait for Renn.

Beyond the firelight a squirrel buried an acorn, patted earth in place, then scampered off. Rip and Rek roosted in an oak with their beaks under their wings. The wolves woke. Yawning and stretching, they padded about, greeting each other with swinging tails and snuffly licks.

Torak watched the stars through the oak's branches. A star shot across the sky and faded like a spark. The others were flickering: that meant a storm on the way. Among them he made out the Great Auroch.

The Great Auroch was the most powerful demon in the Otherworld. In the First Winter it escaped, and the World Spirit fought a terrible battle and flung it burning from the sky. The wind scattered its ashes: little seeds of evil all over the world. Every autumn the Great Auroch rose again. As winter came on it rose higher, glaring at the Forest with its bloodshot red eye – and demons grew stronger...

Renn returned with a birch-bark pail full of puffballs. Sitting beside him, she craned her neck at the sky. 'Do you ever think about when you were flying?'

'Sometimes.'

She looked at him. 'Were you frightened?'

'Yes. But it was amazing too. I miss it.'

The First Tree appeared: immense, slow bursts of green light rippling across the sky.

'It's bright tonight,' said Renn.

Torak put his arm around her. It always comforted him to see the First Tree protecting the Forest.

Wolf lifted his muzzle and howled a welcome to the night. Darkfur joined in, then Pebble, then the cubs' wobbly yowls. Torak put his hands to his mouth and howled with them, thanking the Forest for keeping them safe, and wishing the wolves a good hunt.

Hungry, he went to inspect the firepit.

'You move differently in the Forest,' said Renn.

'Do I?'

'More relaxed. Like a wolf.'

'It's because I'm under trees. I didn't like those huge skies in the Far North.' With a piece of antler he raised a corner of baked mud and breathed a mouthwatering smell of venison. 'Good, I think it's—'

'Have you forgiven me?' Renn said suddenly.

He glanced at her. 'What for?'

'For leaving.'

'Of course I have.'

'Is that the truth?'

He went to her and pulled her to her feet. 'I was angry with you, but not any more. Although – you have to promise me one thing. Promise you'll never, *ever*—'

'I promise.'

'Not good enough, you've got to say it out loud.'

'I promise I'll never ever leave you – without telling you why—'

'No!' He was grinning. 'Promise never to leave!'

In the gloom her white teeth flashed. 'I promise never to leave.' Rising on tiptoe, she kissed him. He kissed her harder. After a while they drew apart.

'Let's eat,' said Torak. 'But remember, all you get is a few bones because you're only a half-man. And you have to walk three steps behind me, and don't—'

He didn't get any further because she was clobbering him and he was laughing and shielding his head with his arms.

Wolf could hear Tall Tailless and the pack-sister yip-and-yowling, which was their way of laughing. Satisfied that all was well, Wolf left the older cub watching the young ones and the taillesses, and he and his mate loped off to hunt.

In the Up, the Tree of Light was singing. Wolf caught the gleam of his mate's eyes in the Dark and the scent of prey on the wind. This was good: it was how it should be.

After a few failed hunts, they killed a young elk and ate till their bellies were taut. Then they trotted back to the Den and sicked it up, and the cubs gobbled the half-chewed meat and fell asleep.

The taillesses were already in their Den. Whatever had been wrong between them was now right. Taillesses were very complicated and much of what they did was a mystery. Wolf didn't understand why the pack-sister had left, but Tall Tailless had forgiven her, so Wolf had too.

It was enough that the pack was together again: that no one had been injured in the hunt; that everyone had eaten their fill. Putting up his muzzle, Wolf howled his happiness to the Forest and to the swaying, singing Tree of Light.

It was good. It was how things should be.

is Torak, Renn and Wolf's

next adventure.

It will be published in April 2021.

Read the first chapter here.

ONE

A Lynx Clan hunter saw it first. He was trudging along a ridge, checking his snares, when he spotted a brilliant spark of light moving fast across the night sky.

The hunter had seen such stars before. He knew they meant the World Spirit was shooting arrows at demons, so he was reassured as he went on his way.

Midwinter, the Dark Time, when the sun is asleep in its cave and doesn't show its face for two whole moons. No wind. Silent pines watching him pass. The only sounds the crunch of his snowshoes, the creak of his reindeer-hide parka and leggings. His breath.

As he approached the next snare he could see as clear as day, thanks to starlight and snowglow, and the rippling green radiance in the sky which the clans call the First Tree.

Good. He'd snared a willow grouse.

The horsehair noose was frozen stiff, so was the bird.

As the hunter stooped to retrieve them, something made him glance up. He was startled to see that the star had grown much brighter, and doubled in size.

*

On the riverbank Renn poked her head out of the shelter. 'Come on, Torak!' she called crossly. 'We need to get going!'

'I'll catch you up!' he replied without turning his head.

'No, you won't, you'll invent an excuse and stay here!'

He blew out a cloud of frosty breath. *Perfect* conditions for ice fishing. He'd hacked four beautiful holes and laid a stick across each one, from which he'd hung his lines and hooks. To attract the fish he'd made torches of folded birch bark jammed in split sticks, and set them in a row. The First Tree was helping too, shining so brightly it was sending the trout crazy, he'd already caught three. Why couldn't he stay here peacefully with the wolves?

Wolf bounded up as if he'd heard Torak's thoughts and licked the frost off his eyebrows. With a grin Torak pushed Wolf's muzzle aside. His thick winter pelt was sprinkled with snow and his breath smelt of fish. It would take too long to tell him in wolf talk that his shadow was spooking the trout, so Torak distracted him by backing away on all fours, uttering eager little grunt-whines: *Let's play!*

Lashing his tail, Wolf went down on his forelegs: *Yes, let's!* Then he pounced, soft-biting his pack-brother's arm with muffled growls and hauling him over the ice.

'You know I'm not leaving without you,' called Renn. In the glare of the torchlight she was a black figure by their shelter, but in his mind Torak saw her red hair tucked behind her ears, her pale, well-loved, infuriatingly stubborn face. 'Dark *wants* us at the Feast,' she insisted.

'Yes, but *why?*'

'I don't know, he said it's important. And he's our friend, and he never asks us for anything!'

Torak tossed a trout onto the far bank and watched Wolf race after it. He heaved a sigh.

The Moon of Long Dark was over and they were into the strange days before Sunwake, when the endless blue night was briefly lightened by a false dawn. The sky would grow pale, as if the sun was about to show itself above the Mountains – only for darkness to return as the sun retreated into its cave.

It was an edgy time when each clan did its best to ensure that in a few days the sun really would rise above the peaks. The Boar Clan burnt a whole spruce tree on a hilltop. Renn's clan, the Ravens, held the Feast of Sparks underground, while their Mage ventured even deeper to kindle the need-fire, and everyone sang and—

'Too many people,' grumbled Torak.

'Oh, Torak, it's not that bad, last winter you enjoyed it!'

He heard the smile in her voice and snorted a laugh. But the holes were freezing over, so he applied himself to clearing them with the butt of his ice scoop, flicking the shards for Wolf's mate, Darkfur: she loved chomping ice.

Wolf lay on the far bank, gripping the half-eaten trout in his forepaws. Behind him on the slope the cubs, Blackpaw and Tug, were pouncing on snowdrifts in futile attempts to catch lemmings. Their older brother Pebble was away guarding the pack's range. As a cub he'd been carried off by an eagle owl, and though he'd grown into a handsome young wolf, the ordeal had marked him, and he rarely relaxed.

Renn was shovelling snow onto the fire with an auroch's shoulder blade. Rip and Rek lit onto the shelter and gurgled a greeting. She gave the ravens a distracted nod. 'It's not as if we've far to go,' she told Torak. 'They're only camped a daywalk away.'

But Torak could be stubborn too. He *liked* the feel of this sleeping valley. The river dreaming under the ice, the alders asleep on its banks. Even the pines were dozing, only a single watch-tree remaining properly awake.

He'd chosen this spot because a family of beavers had dammed the river to make a pool which sheltered many fish. Not far from where he knelt, the beavers' lodge was a mound of blue snow, the air above it faintly quivering from the warmth of the furry bodies snuggled within.

Again he sighed. Renn was right. If Dark really wanted them to come...

'What's that over there?' she said in an altered voice.

He raised his head. 'Where?'

'There.'

She stood facing north, pointing at the sky.

Wolf and Darkfur had seen it too. They stood with ears pricked and tails stiff, bodies rigid with tension.

Slowly Torak rose to his feet.

It was low in the sky above the pines spiking the hilltop: a huge, brilliant, blue-white star.

'It's getting bigger,' said Renn.

*

In the Deep Forest the Lynx Clan hunter stood motionless, his frozen grouse forgotten at his feet. His hand crept to the fur amulet at his throat and under his breath he whispered a prayer to his clan-creature. The star had grown unbearably bright, as big as his fist.

Shielding his eyes with his arms, the hunter lurched against a pine. He heard a strange whistling noise, like a vast flock of geese rushing towards him.

*

The star was brighter than the sun, turning night to dazzling day. Its shadow passed across Torak, he heard a whistling like the rush of enormous wings – then a growl of thunder. 'Get under those rocks!' he yelled to Renn.

Darkfur was streaking across the ice towards her cubs, Renn shouting something he couldn't make out – then the sky was raining fire, a hot wind blowing him off his feet.

He fell with a crash. The ice was heaving, the river waking up. The thunder was louder – but how could there be thunder when there were no clouds?

A stink of singed fur, his parka was on fire. Beating out flames, he struggled to his feet.

He saw pines bending like blades of grass, others flying overhead like spears. On the far bank a blazing poplar had fallen, pinning Wolf to the ground. On the near bank the shelter had collapsed, Torak couldn't see Renn. Next moment he realized that the white thing poking through the wreckage was her hand. Who to help first, Renn or Wolf? *Who?*

A boom like a thousand thunderclaps, swelling to a deafening solid roar...

Silence.

Torak could feel the ice buckling beneath him, see the hillside shaking, trees toppling, boulders crashing – but he couldn't *hear* anything. The Forest was burning, engulfing him in fierce choking smoke.

He could no longer see Renn or Wolf.

*

The Lynx Clan hunter had fallen to his knees. Thunder roaring, trees thrashing, the whole sky on fire—

That was the last thing he ever saw.

The Thunderstar blasted entire valleys to cinders. It turned frozen rivers to raging torrents.

It obliterated the heart of the Forest.

AUTHOR'S NOTE

The world of Torak and Renn is that of six thousand years ago: after the Ice Age, but before farming spread to north-west Europe, when the land was one vast Forest.

The people looked like you or me, but their way of life was very different. They lived in small clans, some staying at a campsite for a few days or moons, others staying put all year round. They didn't have writing, metals or the wheel – but they didn't need them. They were superb survivors. They knew all about the animals, trees, plants and rocks around them. When they wanted something they knew where to find it, or how to make it.

Like the previous books in the series, *Viper's Daughter* takes place in northern Scandinavia. The wildlife which Torak and Renn encounter on their adventures is appropriate to the region, as are the seasonal fluctuations in the hours of daylight. However I've changed mountains, rivers and coastlines to suit the stories, which means that you won't find the specific topography of the Far North or the Forest in a modern atlas.

When I finished *Chronicles of Ancient Darkness*, I was convinced that I would never write a sequel. But the odd thing was that Torak, Renn and Wolf never entirely went away. A few years ago I started wondering what happened to them after the end of the last book. By chance, I'd booked a short break in north Norway. As I tramped through the snowy forest, ideas began to spark; and that night I saw the northern lights pointing north…

To research the story I travelled to the remote Chukotka Peninsula of far eastern Siberia: it's bigger than France, with a population of just a few thousand, and no roads. From there I journeyed by ice-breaker through the Bering Strait to Wrangel Island, the last known refuge of the woolly mammoth. The island was once part of Beringia, the land which bridged Asia and America; and as Wrangel wasn't glaciated, it hasn't changed much since then. I was surprised to find luxuriant vegetation rich in berries and mushrooms. We also came upon a mammoth tusk half-buried in a dry riverbed.

Back in the early 2000s when I began the series, I wasn't aware that mammoths had survived on Wrangel Island until long after Torak and Renn's time. Nor did I know that although the Wrangel mammoths were smaller than their mainland forebears, remains of larger mammoths from about six thousand years ago had been unearthed on the Pribilof Islands. For these reasons I've decided that it isn't too much of a stretch for Torak, Renn and Wolf to encounter mammoths in *Viper's Daughter*.

When we reached Wrangel Island, we found polar bear tracks on every beach we explored – and often we found the bears themselves. Like Torak, I've sat in a small boat (in my case a Zodiac) and glanced up to see a polar bear staring down at me from a clifftop. I've seen one rise from its hiding-place on the shore where I was standing and amble into the sea; and many times I've found it hard to distinguish between driftwood, waves and bears. Nor did I make up Torak's idea of warding them off by imitating the sound of walrus tusks striking rocks. Russian scientists on Wrangel devised this trick, which has worked so well that in forty years they've never had to shoot a bear.

Like Torak and Renn, I've seen a snowy owl hovering perfectly still in winds so strong I could hardly stand. I've paddled under cliffs thronged with seabirds, and got close to snow geese, musk-oxen, walruses and bearded seals. In the Bering Strait I've seen whales in huge numbers, and like Renn I've had a near-miss with a humpback whale. I was on the deck of the ship and the whale surfaced so close to the prow where I was standing that I feared we'd hurt it. Luckily we didn't, but for one unforgettable moment its brown eye met mine.

I didn't make up the island of birds either. In the Bering Strait we came upon a vast 'island' of short-tailed shearwaters feeding on krill churned up by a pod of whales hunting beneath. The island comprised many thousands of tiny voiceless birds, and no one on board, including our guides, had ever seen anything like it. We all felt privileged to watch.

I got ideas for the Narwal Clan from the traditional ways of the Chukchi of Chukotka, who split walrus hides (which are about 6 cm thick) to make their beautiful skinboats, and hunted geese with slingstones (bolas). They also used to give their children the toughest of upbringings so that they would survive the rigours of the Arctic. Like Torak, I've munched tangy roseroot and glossy black smoked whale meat. But I gave *quiviak* (as it's usually spelt) a miss when I came across it in Greenland.

Waigo was inspired by a haunting visit to the abandoned Eskimo* village of Naukan at Cape Dezhnev, where I climbed steep green hills crowned with towering whale-jaw arches and watched sea-fog rolling in. Many other details, such as Naiginn's halibut hook, and the trick of scoring signs on the undersides of bracket mushrooms, I picked up from the Haida and Tlingit people on a visit to Alaska and the islands of Haida Gwaii in British Columbia.

In depicting the volcanic landscape of the Far North, I've drawn on my travels in Iceland and the Aeolian Islands off Sicily, where I explored Vulcano's hissing yellow fumaroles and climbed the ever-active volcano of Stromboli. It was in Chukotka, while I was nosing about downstream of a

---

* The people who lived at Naukan were neither Chukchi nor Inuit; they called themselves Eskimos, and still do.

hot spring wafting sulphurous steam, that I spotted several ready-cooked fish drifting past.

To help me picture the ice cave, I ventured into a huge one beneath the Mendenhall Glacier near Juneau, Alaska. The cave mouth was dangerously unstable and I had to wait for a sign from my guide before darting inside. I couldn't have evoked the roar of the torrent, the vast weight of the glacier overhead, or that otherworldly blue cavern if I hadn't experienced it myself.

As for wolves, I've been a patron of the UK Wolf Conservation Trust since *Wolf Brother* came out in 2004, until it closed to the public and the wolves went into well-deserved retirement, in 2018. Over the years I've cherished the wolves' foibles and their different characters, which continue to provide inspiration for the new books.

*

Now I need to thank some people, including the crews and guides of: the *Professor Khromov* (aka *The Spirit of Enderby*), on which I journeyed from Anadyr to Wrangel Island in 2015; the *Island Roamer*, on which I explored Haida Gwaii; and the *Wilderness Adventurer* in Alaska, on which I spent time in Alaska's Inside Passage and Glacier Bay National Park. It's been a joy to work once more with the two artists who made the original *Chronicles of Ancient Darkness* books so beautiful, and I want to thank Geoff Taylor for his gorgeously evocative chapter illustrations and endpaper maps, and John Fordham for his stunning cover design.

As ever, very special thanks go to my agent, Peter Cox, for his inexhaustible enthusiasm for these stories, his dauntless support and his original thinking. Finally, I am deeply grateful to Fiona Kennedy, my marvellous editor and publisher, who has lived and breathed Torak's world from the beginning. Without her talent and commitment I would not have contemplated writing *Viper's Daughter*.

Michelle Paver,
London 2019

michellepaver.com
wolfbrother.com

Run Wild with Wolf Brother, but first find your Clan.

Where do you belong in Torak's world?

1. What moon were you born under?

If you are born in the first half of February you're born under the Willow Grouse Moon. If you are born in the second half of February you are born under the Moon of Green Snow. However, if you are born in the middle you can take your pick!

Moons in Torak's time aren't fixed to specific dates, the way our calendar months are; they change with the moon.

Jan – Sun-Wake Moon
Feb – Willow Grouse Moon/ Moon of Green Snow
Mar – Moon of Roaring Rivers
Apr – Birchblood Moon
May – Moon of the Salmon Run

Jun – Moon of No Dark
Jul – Cloudberry Moon
Aug – Moon of Green Ashseed
Sep – Moon of Roaring Stags
Oct – Blackthorn Moon
Nov – Moon of Red Willow
Dec – Moon of Long Dark

2. Shelters

It is a cold, crisp morning. Members from each clan have started arriving at the mouth of the Elk River. Everyone knows that the first rule of camping is never to leave it too late to build a shelter. It's time to build yours. What does your shelter look like?

a. An open-fronted shelter with a reindeer-hide roof sloping down to the ground. A cross-beam across the top deflects smoke from the fire in front of the shelter, and traps the warmth inside.
b. Built on a forest of log stilts over water, with wooden platforms on top bearing squat, domed reed shelters.
c. Humped grey seal hides over a whale-rib frame.
d. One large shelter of reindeer hide stained green. Everyone in your clan sleeps inside.
e. One large humped shelter of black and white seal hide; everyone in your clan sleeps inside. This is your

clan's summer/autumn shelter; the winter one is made of snow, but Elk River isn't far enough north.

f. Several sleds propped together and draped with reindeer hides which are weighted with stones. This is only a temporary shelter as you're too tired to make a more lasting one.

3. Trading

Now the shelters are made, people begin to lay out items to trade. You walk through the camp marvelling at the different treasures. You have an old knife to trade, what do you swap it for?

a. Necklace of reindeer teeth.
b. Beaver tooth knife.
c. Blue flint knife with kelp handle.
d. Soap made of ash mixed with burnt green bracken.
e. A small swansfoot pouch made from scaly feet skin, with the claws still attached.
f. Amulet of smoky crystal.

4. Food

As you walk around your stomach starts to rumble. There are so many new smells from foods that you have never tasted before. What will you decide to eat?

a. Auroch-gut sausage with a delicious mix of marrow fat, blood and crushed hazelnut.
b. Reed-pollen cakes with stewed trout and bog mushrooms.
c. Baked marshmallow roots, grey seal stew and chewy dried cod.
d. Roast wood pigeons with flatcakes of crushed hazelnuts and pine pollen, covered in honey.
e. Sweet mash of seal fat and cloudberries with whale skin and frozen seal.
f. Stewed willow grouse with reindeer marrow and tongues, mashed cloudberries and heather tea.

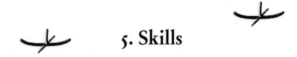

5. Skills

You are surrounded by so many new people from different clans, each of them skilled in different things according to their way of life. You see them exchanging tips and advice and want to join in. What skills do you have to share?

a. Hunting and tracking with stealth and respect.
b. Weaving reeds to create beautiful mats, clothes and boats.
c. Building the best skinboats that skim the waves perfectly.
d. An unsurpassed knowledge and affinity with your

surroundings enabling you to forage for the best materials to make tools and clothes.

e. Driving dogsleds faster and more skilfully than any other clan.

f. Scaling rock faces with speed and agility.

6. Boats

You have built a shelter, traded, shared your skills and sampled some amazing new food. Now it's time to play. Someone calls, 'first to the other edge of the riverbank wins some forest horse meat!'. Everyone runs to their boats, hopping in and paddling frantically. Quick – choose a boat and join the fun:

a. A deer-hide canoe over a willow frame, lashed together with spruce root.

b. A reed boat curved at the prow and stern, like a waterbird.

c. A long, slender, very light skinboat made of grey seal hide, covered at prow and stern.

e. A light canoe of reindeer rawhide.

f. A big sturdy skinboat of dehaired seal hide over a whalebone frame.

g. Smaller, rounded reindeer hide craft.

7. Clan-Tattoos

Your day has been exciting but dusk is now falling. As the moon starts to rise, it is time for you to prepare for the night-time gathering of the clans. You look at your name-soul in a puddle. What clan-tattoos do you see?

a. Three fine blue-black bars on your cheekbones.
b. Undulating blue-green waves up your throat.
c. Wavy blue tattoos on your calves if you're a girl; on your arms if you're a boy.
d. A small black cloven hoof on your forehead.
e. A broad black band across your nose.
f. Thirteen small red dots in a ring on your forehead.

8. Clothes

Having checked your clan-tattoos, you check your clothes. After a long day spent exploring and trading, you need to dust them off and repair any holes. You are ready! Now as you check your name-soul in a puddle, what clothes are you wearing?

a. A deer-hide parka and leggings with beaver-hide boots.
b. A silvery fishskin jerkin and leggings, fringed at neck, hem and sleeves to look like reeds. Your earlobes are

pierced by tiny carved bone fish hooks.

c. Grey seal-hide clothes with a light see-through gutskin parka on top; your long hair is beaded with tiny shells and fishbones.

d. A roe deer buckskin jerkin and leggings lined with hare fur; elk-hide boots; a supple cape of woven nettlestem.

d. A silver sealskin parka and leggings, boots of dehaired seal hide criss-crossed with braided sinew.

e. A reindeer-hide parka and leggings, lined with felted musk-ox wool. White feathers tied to the tip of your hood.

9. Clan Meet

Welcome to the night-time gathering of the clans. The Moon of Roaring Stags is high in the sky. All the clans have gathered. Each will stand up and name themselves. You are nervous, this is your first meet. This will be the moment you are officially acknowledged by all the Clan Leaders. Fin-Kedinn rises from his seat and looks at you.

Which is your clan?

Turn the page to find out.

Mostly As:

Welcome to the Raven Clan!

Like all the Raven Clan you are practical, observant, tolerant and an excellent communicator.

Here are some facts about your new home…

- Shelter: An open–fronted shelter with a reindeer-hide roof sloping down to the ground. A cross-beam across the top deflects smoke from the fire in front of the shelter, and traps the warmth inside.
- Special treasure: Necklace of reindeer teeth.
- Food: Auroch-gut sausage with a delicious mix of marrow fat, blood and crushed hazelnut.
- Skills: Hunting and tracking with stealth and respect.
- Boat: A deer-hide canoe over a willow frame, lashed together with spruce roots.
- Clan-tattoos: Three fine blue-black bars on your cheekbones.
- Clothes: A deer-hide parka and leggings with beaver hide boots.

Mostly Bs:

Welcome to the Otter Clan!

Like all the Otter Clan you're independent, happy to be different and go your own way.

Here are some facts about your new home...

- Shelter: Built on a forest of log stilts over water, with wooden platforms on top bearing squat, domed reed shelters.
- Special treasure: Beaver tooth knife.
- Food: Reed pollen cakes with stewed trout and bog mushrooms.
- Skills: Weaving reeds to create beautiful mats, clothes and boats.
- Boat: A reed boat curved at the prow and stern, like a waterbird.
- Clan-tattoos: Undulating blue-green waves up your throat.
- Clothes: A silvery fishskin jerkin and leggings, fringed at neck, hem and sleeves to look like reeds. Your earlobes are pierced by tiny carved bone fish hooks.

Mostly Cs:

Welcome to the Seal Clan!

Like all the Seal Clan you are proud and graceful, a keen observer of the wind, weather and Sea.

Here are some facts about your new home...

- Shelter: Humped grey seal hides over a whale-rib frame.
- Special Treasure: Blue flint knife with kelp handle.
- Food: Baked marshmallow roots, grey seal stew and chewy dried cod.
- Skills: Building the best skinboats that skim the waves perfectly.
- Boat: A long, slender, very light skinboat made of grey seal hide, covered at prow and stern.
- Clan-tattoos: Wavy blue tattoos on your calves if you're a girl; on your arms if you're a boy.
- Clothes: Grey seal-hide clothes with a light see-through gutskin parka on top; your long hair is beaded with tiny shells and fishbones.

Mostly Ds:

Welcome to the Red Deer Clan!

Like all the Red Deer Clan you are solitary and deeply attuned to the Forest.

Here are some facts about your new home...

- Shelter: One large shelter of reindeer hide stained green. Everyone in your clan sleeps inside.
- Special treasure: Soap made of ash mixed with burnt green bracken.
- Food: Roast wood pigeons with flatcakes of crushed hazelnuts and pine pollen, covered in honey.
- Skills: An unsurpassed knowledge and affinity with your surroundings enabling you to forage for the best materials to make tools and clothes.
- Boat: A light canoe of reindeer rawhide.
- Clan-tattoos: A small black cloven hoof on your forehead.
- Clothes: A roe deer buckskin jerkin and leggings lined with hare fur; elk-hide boots; a supple cape of woven nettlestem.

Mostly Es:

Welcome to the White Fox Clan!

Like all the White Fox Clan you are sociable and love to talk and laugh. You're also exceptionally tough!

Here are some facts you about your new home...

- Shelter: One large humped shelter of black and white seal hide; everyone in your clan sleeps inside. This is your clan's summer/autumn shelter; the winter one is made of snow, but Elk River isn't far enough north.
- Special treasure: A small swansfoot pouch made from scaly feet skin, with the claws still attached.
- Food: Sweet mash of seal fat and cloudberries with whale skin and frozen seal.
- Skills: Driving dogsleds faster and more skilfully than any other clan.
- Boat: A big sturdy skinboat of dehaired seal hide over a whalebone frame.
- Clan-tattoos: A broad black band across your nose.
- Clothes: A silver sealskin parka and leggings, boots of dehaired seal hide criss-crossed with braided sinew.

Mostly Fs:

Welcome to the Swan Clan!

Like all the Swan Clan you're practical, resilient and sharply aware of the spirits in all things.

Here are some facts about your new home...

- Shelter: Several sleds propped together and draped with reindeer hides which are weighted with stones. This is only a temporary shelter as you're too tired to make a more lasting one.
- Special treasure: Amulet of smoky crystal.
- Food: Stewed willow grouse with reindeer marrow and tongues, mashed cloudberries and heather tea.
- Skills: Scaling rock faces with speed and agility.
- Boat: Smaller, rounded reindeer hide craft.
- Clan tattoos: Thirteen small red dots in a ring on your forehead.
- Clothes: A reindeer hide parka and leggings, lined with felted musk-ox wool. White feathers tied to the tip of your hood.